REVENGE

THE ELEVENTH PETE CULNANE MYSTERY

S.L. Smith

SIGHTLINE PRESS

St. Paul, Minnesota

ISBN: 979-8-9868405-4-3

First Edition, February 2026

Printed in the United States of America

Cover design by Christopher Smith

SIGHTLINE PRESS
St. Paul, Minnesota 55117
www.slsmithbooks.com

For all the friends who have added so much to my life. You have kept me going through good times and challenges.

ONE

The Phone Call

When the phone rang and his wife yelled from the kitchen that it was Dave, Brian Barrett threw up his hands in exasperation. He and his three kids were sprawled out on the family room floor, immersed in conquering the Star Wars Millennium Falcon, one of the largest LEGO sets. Ever since his kids became teenagers, quality time with them was at a premium.

Unfortunately, when in trouble, Brian's brother Dave always turned to him, and this was no exception.

Hanging up, Brian looked apologetically at his kids and said, "Gotta go. Dave needs me."

The kids groaned, and his youngest flung a LEGO at the wall with all his might.

Understanding his son's frustration, Brian didn't chastise him. He just grabbed his jacket and car keys and walked out the door. To protect his kids, he waited until he reached his car to call his other brother, Jack. He needed Jack's calming and stabilizing influence to keep from ripping Dave apart when he reached him.

Brian had no idea that, in less than fifteen hours, bailing Dave out of jail would be the worst mistake of his life ... and Dave's.

Jack answered, saying, "You know dinner time with my wife is sacred."

"I do, but obviously Dave doesn't ... or doesn't care."

"Tell me he hasn't been drinking."

"Are you trying to make a liar out of me?"

"When did they arrest him and where?" Jack asked.

"I didn't ask. He begged me to bail him out and, angry as I am, I couldn't say no. Don't you remember, in college I got an F- in tough love?"

"At least you're able to laugh, rather than swearing a blue streak. Does this call mean you want *me* to bail him out?"

"No, I want you to come along while I do, so I'm not arrested for assault."

"Are you going to pick me up or meet me there? And which one of us is going to spend the night with him, then get him to the arraignment?"

"We'll flip a coin. Let's meet at the Ramsey County Jail. That'll reduce the time involved for one of us. Willing, Jack?"

"I'm leaving now. See you there in about thirty minutes. I wish he appreciated us at least a little."

"Someday, perhaps," Brian said, then disconnected, and started his car.

As soon as he reached the interstate, Jack called Brian back. "We need to figure out how to handle this," he said.

"Are you giving up on AA?" Brian asked.

"Dave and I just spoke the day before yesterday," Jack said. "I always try to call him on Sundays, thinking that without Melissa, Sundays may be especially hard for him. He bragged that he'd been dry for almost two months. The last time, he made it for almost three. The time before that was also about three months. Do you see a pattern here?"

"You know it'll continue unless we can get him on a new path," Brian said.

2

By the time they reached the Ramsey County Jail, they'd decided to have Dave committed to Hazelden Betty Ford Clinic. They debated letting him sleep it off in jail, but decided they couldn't deliver that kind of one-two punch. Unfortunately, both brothers were oblivious to the fact that would have been the best thing they could have done for him.

Hearing the charges came as a blow. Dave wasn't arrested for DUI or for drunk and disorderly conduct. Minus his two front teeth, he was stone-cold sober when they cuffed him, dragged him to the jail, and booked him on charges of assault.

Jack and Brian both felt ashamed for jumping to the wrong conclusions. Both offered to spend the night with him.

With cracked lips and a swollen mouth, Dave looked like the stereotypical street brawler. Jack and Brian felt sick when Dave's smile revealed the space once occupied by his beautiful, white, front teeth.

"Do you have them?" Brian asked.

"As soon as the cops succeeded in pulling Cam off me, I tried to find them, but they cuffed me and dragged me away. Tried telling them I needed to find my teeth. They ignored me."

His brothers decided not to ask for the details, at least until they reached more comfortable surroundings. They drove Dave downtown to the Robert Street ramp to pick up his car. While there, they viewed the scene of the brawl and searched for his teeth—even though all three knew it was too late to do anything but put them under his pillow and hope for a visit from the tooth fairy.

They drove all three cars to Dave's home. Once they settled in the dining room, Dave explained how and why

Cameron Remer jumped him as he got out of the elevator on his floor of the parking ramp.

Having assumed the worst, Brian and Jack felt like jerks. They each offered to spend the next few nights with Dave or take him home with them.

But Dave wanted to be alone. He wanted to call his attorney, put an icepack on his mouth, and go to bed. "I want to look well rested and in control for the arraignment. Knowing Cam the way I do, he'll cook up a story for his attorney that would bring Ma Barker to tears. I'm contemplating the best way to give the judge a glimpse at my missing teeth." He smiled, as best he could in light of the swelling.

At 8:00 on Wednesday morning, Jack and Brian sat in the Ramsey County Courthouse with Dave's attorney, Joel Milroy, wondering where Dave was. Joel and Dave had planned to arrive ahead of schedule, giving them time to confer beforehand. The anxiety level grew with each passing minute.

"I called him this morning," Jack said. "He'd already showered. He was right on schedule. He sounded a little nervous but otherwise fine. Could he have been in an accident?"

"The thing is," Brian said, "except when he's drinking, he's always punctual." Having been so wrong last night, Brian refused to consider that possibility.

Finally, lacking a better option, Jack extracted his cellphone from a pants pocket and called Dave's cell. After four rings, the call went to voicemail.

"Dead battery?" Brian asked.

"No way. I plugged it in for him last night. Do you think he forgot to grab it on his way out the door? I'm sure he had a lot on his mind."

"Why don't the two of you sit tight, and I'll go look for him," Brian said.

"You know what will happen if you do," Dave's attorney said. "As soon as you leave, he'll walk in. Hang tough a while longer."

Five minutes later, with still no sign of Dave, Brian stood and said, "I can't just sit here. I'll drive to his house via the route he'd probably take and look for him. If I don't find him, I'll check his house. What if something happened to him? I have to find out. When he arrives and proves all this worrying was for nothing, call me."

Jack nodded. He didn't tell Brian that for the last forty-five minutes, things hadn't felt right. Unlike Brian, rather than acting on those fears, he stayed in the courthouse and prayed.

Two
Intercepted

Hearing the distinct gait, Commander Peter Culnane, an investigator with the St. Paul PD, glanced up from his desk. Until now, the reports required to close out his and Martin's most recent case had his undivided attention. Few things could change that, aside from Senior Commander Lincoln, his boss and the head of the Homicide Unit. Pete sighed, certain he knew what this meant.

He was spot on.

He stood as Commander Lincoln entered his office.

Grim faced, Lincoln said, "Grab Martin. There was a shooting on the East Side, in the Phalen-Payne neighborhood, across the street from Lake Phalen. One man is dead. Forensics is on the way."

"Yes, Sir," Pete said. Grabbing his suit coat, he hurried out of his office.

Lincoln called after him, "I'll let Forensics know when we have a search warrant for the victim's home."

In search of Martin, Pete nearly collided with him as he rounded a corner.

Martin jumped back and said, "Just heard. East side?"

Pete nodded, and they rushed to Martin's unmarked car in the parking lot at headquarters. With Martin still

6

panting from trying to keep up with Pete's long stride, they pulled out of the lot, heading for northbound I-35E.

It was nearly 9:00 a.m., and they were leaving rather than approaching downtown St. Paul, so rush hour traffic didn't impede Martin's lead foot. Nevertheless, he proceeded cautiously, with flashing lights but without the siren. They followed I-35E to the Wheelock Parkway/Larpenteur Avenue exit. Then they took Wheelock east. The parkway was appropriately named, due to the stretches of densely wooded areas. Houses along the way dated back to the 1920s, 1930s, and 1940s, and they ranged from well-maintained to a bit less so.

As soon as they crossed Arcade Street, the Phalen Golf Course encompassed the northern side of the road, while a recreation center and baseball diamonds occupied the south side. A bit further down the road, one- and two-story houses stood on the right, with a tree-filled boulevard separating them from Wheelock.

On the left, past the golf course and approaching Lake Phalen, sat a park, then the lake. The trees attempted but failed to hide the lake from motorists on Wheelock. Shortly after Martin turned left onto East Shore Drive, the trees on their left and right provided the illusion of driving through a dense forest. On the right, in combination with the underbrush, the trees grew so thick, they hid what lay behind them. It was mid-September, but only a few leaves showed signs of orange and yellow.

Still several hundred feet from their destination, they saw the swarm of police cars and flashing lights. Closing the distance, on the street end of a driveway, they saw a man wearing a suit and another in dress slacks and a

7

sport coat. They appeared on the verge of coming to blows with two uniformed officers.

Arms flailing, the men screamed at the officers. Feet planted and hands on their duty belts, the officers screamed right back.

Before Martin could pull over to the side of the road, Pete jumped out and dashed to the impending fracas, remembering the opening lines of a poem by Rudyard Kipling, "If you can keep your head when all about you are losing theirs ..." *In this case, that's an overstatement,* he thought, *and the rest of the poem isn't applicable. But keeping that principle in mind has served me well.*

Pete heard the men in street clothes scream, "That's our brother. You can't keep us out! We have a *right* to be with him. You have to let us be with him!"

He sprinted the remaining distance and moved in close. But he wasn't foolish enough to plant himself between the two groups. He said calmly and barely louder than a whisper, "Take a deep breath, everyone, and let's talk."

Jaws clenched and red-eyed, the men in street clothes looked at him furiously. Pete studied them. They appeared to be in their mid- to late-forties. Strong resemblances, including above average height, slender build, broad shoulders, thick dark hair transitioning to gray, and thin-lipped mouths suggested the family connection. One wore a navy Ralph Lauren suit. The other wore dress slacks and a navy sport coat.

As the men took deep breaths, struggling to regain control, Pete said, "Let's start with your names."

"I'm Jack Barrett," the man in a sport coat who appeared a year or two younger said.

"I'm Brian," the other said.

"Now, what's the problem?" Pete asked.

"Are you deaf and blind?" Jack demanded. "That's our brother up there on the garage floor, and they won't let me near him. I need to hold his hand and touch his face. I need to tell him I love him! Brian had the chance. *I didn't!* You can't stop me! I *have* to do it while his spirit is still hovering."

"Please, whoever you are," Brian pled, "can't they stop long enough to let him do that? Despite the line they're giving us, it *can't* hurt anything."

The two uniformed officers moved off to the side as Pete introduced himself and Martin before saying, "My heart goes out to both of you. Your request seems reasonable, and you might not disturb the crime scene, but you might. So it could mean the difference between finding and not finding the person who did this. Rather than standing here, let's walk to the unmarked car and talk."

"I have a key, so why not talk in Dave's house?" Jack asked.

"Because for the time being, it's part of the crime scene."

Pete looked up at the house he now knew belonged to the victim. It stood at the top of an incline and about twenty feet above the street. The gradient limited his view of the overall crime scene.

He noted the house was two stories with gray stone on the first floor and gray cedar shake siding on the second. On the left side stood an attached, two-car garage. A royal blue BMW sat in the center, occupying both stalls, and emergency workers gathered around a body between the driver's side door of the BMW and the wall.

An abundance of mature trees, shrubs, and flower beds, surrounded by dark-gray pavers, gave the yard a lush appearance. This lot and those on both sides seemed large enough to accommodate a football field, if you eliminated the house and the end zones.

Walking toward the unmarked car, Pete told Jack, "It sounds like you believe in an afterlife. I do, and I believe if your brother's here, he knows what you're thinking and feeling, even though you aren't right there with him. After the medical examiner and crime scene folks finish, you'll have a chance to be with him. Right now, there's no way of knowing what trace evidence is near or on his body, clothes, or the garage floor. Did you move him after you found him?" he asked Brian.

With a cracking, strained voice, Brian said, "No. I found him face down. I touched his cheek and spoke to him, hoping he was still alive. I already told them all about it," he said, motioning back over his shoulder toward the garage and the ME and crime scene crews.

Pete asked, "Any idea who did this?"

"Maybe the guy who beat him up last night," Jack said. "We bailed him out of jail. He was supposed to meet us downtown this morning for his arraignment." Gesturing toward his brother he said, "This is probably our fault. He wouldn't have been here had we left him in jail."

Brian put an arm around Jack, and the two men sobbed.

After a respectful pause, Martin said, "You said Dave was supposed to be arraigned this morning. What were the charges?"

"I'm not sure," Brian said. "It sounded like brawling or maybe assault. Either way, he didn't start it. He was just trying to defend himself. He told us about it last night, when we brought him home."

"The other guy, Cameron Remer," Brian continued, "knocked out Dave's front teeth. Dave didn't think Cameron was injured. Regardless, the guy attacked Dave. Like I said, Dave was just defending himself."

"But they were both charged?" Martin asked.

"Yeah," Jack said. "Nice, huh?"

"What's the connection between your brother and Remer?" Pete asked.

"Dave is ... was an accountant. Remer was a client, and he freaked out over an IRS audit. He blamed Dave, claimed he must have screwed something up. Dave said he discovered Remer failed to provide a 1099 for a new investment account. Because it was a new account, without that 1099, Dave had no way of knowing about it."

"Since Remer was arrested last night," Pete said, "we can get his contact information. Do you know or have you met him?"

The brothers shook their heads.

"Did you see him at the courthouse this morning?" Martin asked. "Did he arrive before you left to come here?"

"No," Brian said, "but I left quite some time before he had to be there."

"I didn't see him either," Jack said. "He was dead-lining it by not being there before I left. Do you think he came here and killed Dave before going to the courthouse?"

To be determined, thought Pete and Martin, and Martin said, "We'll see where the investigation takes us."

Rain was predicted, but for now it was partly cloudy and 76° F. Taking advantage of an unseasonably warm September morning, the four men decided to move to the shade of a large red maple, preparing to lose its luster.

"Does Dave have an office or did he work from home?" Pete asked.

"He has an office on the mezzanine level in the Golden Rule Building downtown," Jack said.

"What time did you get here?" Martin asked.

"About 8:45," Brian said. "Came looking for Dave. We were worried when he didn't arrive at the courthouse way past the time we'd agreed to meet there. As I approached the house, I saw the garage door was open and the BMW was inside. I didn't see Dave until I started driving up the driveway." Brian brushed away a tear.

"What time did you plan to meet at the courthouse?" Martin asked.

"At 8:00," Jack said.

"So he should have left here by 7:30?" Martin asked.

Again, both brothers nodded.

"Did you call 911?" Pete asked Brian.

Brian sniffed and said, "Called as soon as I saw him on the garage floor. Then ran to him, touched his face and hand, got an ear as close as I could to his face, hoping to hear him breathing. I didn't hear anything, but I said his name several times, hoping. Called Jack right away, but the police and paramedics arrived before he did, of course."

"Does anyone else live here?" Martin asked, thinking it was a big house for one person and wondering why no one had emerged to check on all the commotion.

"Dave lived alone," Jack sighed. "His wife passed more than a year ago. At least she didn't have to go through this."

"Did your brother ever mention problems with anyone besides Remer?" Pete asked. "Anyone he had issues with? Anyone who concerned or threatened him?"

"No," Brian said. "Until last night, we didn't even know about Remer."

"Who are his friends?" Pete asked.

"We mentioned that his wife, Melissa, died," Brian said. "That was thirteen months ago. She was his best friend, the love of his life, and the center of his universe. They did everything together, and he fell apart when she died. Then he turned to and found solace in alcohol. Jack and I finally convinced him to join AA. He may have some friends there, but I don't know where the meetings were conducted or the name of his sponsor. Do you, Jack?"

Jack bit his lip and shook his head.

"Dave is six years younger than me and almost five years younger than Jack," Brian continued. "So other than his college roommate, who was also his best man, I don't know any of his friends, do you, Jack?"

Again Jack shook his head.

"What's his best man's name?" Martin asked.

"Mike Hinckley," Jack said.

"Do you have his contact information?" Martin asked.

"I just know he lives out east," Jack said. "Maryland, I think."

"Where did they go to college?" Martin asked.

"Macalester College," Jack said.

"How about coworkers?" Pete asked.

"None," Jack said. "He was a one-person operation."

"Your parents?" Pete asked.

"Dad died five years ago," Jack said. "Mom remarried and moved to France with the guy. I never hear from her. Do you, Brian?"

Brian shook his head and said, "She didn't even come home for Melissa's funeral. Dave never said, but I doubt he was speaking to her."

"Are Melissa's parents still alive?" Martin asked.

Both brothers nodded, and Brian said, "Their names are Tim and Dorothy Peterson. They remained close to Dave after Melissa's death, and live in a senior community in Inver Grove Heights."

They also learned Melissa had an older brother, Matt, and a younger sister, Amy Campbell. Brian and Jack claimed ignorance when it came to Dave's relationship to them. Even so, at Dave's request, Jack had them in the contacts on his cellphone and shared that information with Pete and Martin.

"Was Dave a golfer, active in his church, a member of any associations?" Pete asked.

Both brothers responded with a hands-up shrug and "Sorry."

"His computer might be helpful," Martin said. "Do you know if he had one at work and one at home?"

Their heads shook.

"They're probably password protected," Martin said. "Any idea what he used or might have used as a password?"

"I know Melissa's birthday is the passcode on his phone, so it could be her birthday ... or her name ... or their anniversary."

"Do you know those dates?" Martin asked.

"Yup," Jack sighed. "She was born on December 20, 1978. The date is easy to remember, because it's so close to Christmas, and she was born a year after Dave. Sorry, that's probably way too much information."

"Wedding date?" Martin asked.

"They got married on my birthday," Brian explained. June 24 ... 2000."

The two investigators obtained the sparse details the brothers could provide about Melissa's parents, brother, sister, and friends.

"Have any neighbors come over to ask what's going on?" Pete asked.

"I haven't noticed any, but I've been kinda preoccupied," Brian said sarcastically. He kicked a pine cone and added, "I'd imagine they're all at work. Met some of them when Melissa was ill, and they all came to her funeral. They loved her. She was charismatic and a real social butterfly. They are all couples in their forties, both with careers, and their kids would have been in or on their way to school before this happened. Besides, the yards are huge and there's only Lake Phalen across the street."

Pete often ran to and around Lake Phalen, and he'd noticed this row of attractive homes whose sprawling yards provided an unusual degree of privacy. Experience also indicated, aside from the early morning diehards, few walkers or runners used the walking paths around the lake before midmorning. Both groups tended to concentrate on the lake, the winding path, and booby traps like low hanging or downed branches and rocks, as well as the completion of their workouts.

That means, Pete thought, *anyone targeting Dave Barrett or his home had few impediments ... and it wouldn't take a genius to circumvent them.*

"You spent some time with your brother last night," Pete said. "I understand he was about to be arraigned but, try to put that aside. Did he seem more anxious, nervous, or preoccupied than normal? Did it seem like something else was bothering or worrying him?"

"I have no idea," Brian said. "He was exhausted. If there was something, he didn't mention it."

"Knowing him the way you did," Pete said, "if there was something, would he have mentioned it?"

"Maybe, but not definitely," Brian said.

"I agree with Brian," Jack said. "So I called him about 7:00 this morning to check on him and make sure he was up and moving. He was anxious and keyed, but I figured that was about his arraignment. He didn't let on about anything else."

Or he suspected someone was coming after him and didn't want to endanger your lives by getting you involved, Pete thought.

"Did he belong to a church or regularly attend services?" he asked, looking for a starting point from which to try tracking down Dave's AA attendance.

"He got married in the Catholic church just east of here," Brian said. "I don't know if he still belonged or attended Masses."

Pete knew the church he referenced and made a note to speak with the pastor.

"Are you employed?" Pete asked the brothers.

"Yes," Brian said. "I'm a VP at 3M."

"And I'm a dentist with my own practice," Jack said.

Pete and Martin obtained Brian's address in Forest Lake and his phone numbers, as well as Jack's phone numbers and address in Apple Valley. They gave the brothers their business cards and asked to be notified if they heard anything or thought of anything ... or anyone ... who might be helpful.

16

"We'll speak with the medical examiner and Forensics next," Pete said. "We know you're anxious to see your brother. We'll try to shorten your wait."

That was important to Pete, but it obviously wasn't his top priority for that meeting.

THREE
The Crime Scene

The two investigators approached Dave Barrett's garage. They wanted every iota of information currently available from the Ramsey County ME and the St. Paul PD's Forensics Services Unit regarding Dave Barrett's last moments.

Both had already noted the location and position of the body. As Brian said, Dave lay face down. It looked like he'd nearly made it to the driver's side door. They saw the soles of his shoes, toes down, by the rear, driver's side wheel. It seemed he'd crumbled without reacting to or breaking his fall, as his face collided with the garage floor, near the driver's side mirror.

No doubt they rolled him over, Pete thought, *but if that approximates the way they found him, it appears the person who killed him snuck up on him and he had no idea what was happening.*

The Ramsey County ME, in the person of Don, their lead investigator, provided even more information than Pete and Martin dared hope.

"He was hit in the back of the head," Don said, "and there were fragments of a paver and a few clumps of dirt alongside his body. After the autopsy, Forensics will check to see if they match anything we find on his scalp or in his hair."

"Appears he died instantly. When we arrived, he lay face down, hands at his sides. Turning him over, we saw he wore a look of utter surprise."

"Indications are," Don continued, "he didn't react to the person coming up behind him. Either that person was mighty stealthy or they got behind him while the garage door was still on its way up, drowning out the sound of their approach. Or maybe he was distracted. Unfortunately, you could eat off this garage floor, so the victim didn't benefit from the sound of crunching leaves or sand grinding into the cement."

Martin leaned toward Pete and whispered, "Let that be a lesson to you. Then he turned to Don and said, "I see you bagged the victim's hands. Based on what you just said, there's no chance he got some of the attacker's skin under his nails."

Adding to the picture, Gary from Forensics asked, "As you approached, did you notice the huge shrub just right of the garage door? Behind it looks like a perfect spot to hide while waiting for the garage door to go up. And there's a missing paver towards the back, where you'd have to examine the area to see it. It might be the murder weapon, and the attacker may have taken the rest of it along to make our job more difficult. It appears they used a flathead screwdriver or something similar to dislodge it. Finding someone in possession of whatever was used with remnants of that soil would be helpful." He smirked.

"Unfortunately," he added, "we didn't find any footprints in here. That could be thanks to all the mulch around that bush. It's possible there are fibers from the shooter's socks, slacks, shirt, jacket, etcetera, in the mulch or bush. Too bad it's too warm for sweats; they more readily shed fibers. But the top brands are so popular, they no longer provide much of a lead."

"We lifted fingerprints from all the exterior door handles and the garage door opener button," Gary continued. "But if our suspicions are correct and the person waited for the victim to put up the garage door then attacked him and took off through the still open door, it's unlikely we'll come up with anything. However, after the attack, maybe they stood over him, looking down at their handiwork, and shed a few hairs." Gary grinned.

"Ever the optimist," Don said, rolling his eyes.

"Wonder why it took them so long to reach and attack him," Gary noted. "If they hid behind that bush, they should have been able to reach him before he got to the BMW. Were they bent on anonymity? If they planned to murder and not just injure him, why was that important? Did they suspect he carried a weapon? Did they believe he could best them if he saw them? Are they so large, out of shape, or disabled that it took that long to reach him? Was attacking him from behind important or symbolic? The answers could be important."

"Duly noted," Pete said. He'd wondered the same things.

Pointing to the shelves in the front and along the right side of the garage, Gary said, "The garage is loaded with sound-absorbing materials, like what has to be at least a dozen packing blankets. Had he seen someone coming and screamed, they would have helped reduce the sound. In combination with the oversized lots, it may have kept anyone from hearing anything ... not that it appears there was much to hear."

"We don't have a search warrant yet," he said. "I'm anxious to search the house for anything that could help us or you."

"We got some info that might help, once you get the warrant," Pete said. "His brothers told us his wife's birthday is the passcode for his phone, and they think he probably used her name, birthday, or their wedding date for some of his passwords." Flipping to the right page in his notepad, he recited those things.

"We have the phone," Gary said and requested a text containing the name and numbers.

"In return," Pete said, "as soon as you can get to it, we'd like the victim's contact information from his computer and cellphone, as well as a list of the names and phone numbers he contacted or who contacted him in the last two weeks. You never know ... By the way," he added, "the brothers are standing at the end of the driveway. Seeing him is important to them. I'm sure you understand. Please do whatever you can to accommodate."

Don and Gary nodded, and Don said, "I'll go get them in just a few minutes."

Then testing the waters, Pete said, "The victim and another man were arrested yesterday, and his brothers said it was for brawling or assault."

Simultaneously, Don and Gary said, "They don't know which?"

"Or so they say," Pete said. "They said their brother claimed he took the brunt of the blows, but it's possible the other man wasn't yet finished with him."

"And you suspect the other man?" Gary asked.

"I want to talk to him," Pete said.

"It would take an idiot to kill him when, thanks to the fight, there's already a flashing red arrow pointing at him," Gary said.

"If good sense or logic typically won out over emotions," Pete said, "I'd agree. How many cases do you know where it wasn't that way?"

"As in the fact that our prisons are crowded with those people?" Gary asked.

"Exactly." Pete nodded.

FOUR

A Bonus Sandwiched In

"**W**ant to go to confession?" Pete asked Martin as they hoofed their way back to Martin's unmarked car.

Eyebrows raised, Martin asked, "As in, forgive me Pete, for I have sinned?"

"No thanks, Martin. There aren't enough hours in the day for even a condensed version. Plus, I haven't the stomach to hear your sins, nor the power to forgive them." Pete laughed.

"When you were a kid, did you want to be a priest, Pete?"

"Nope. I had my heart set on a career in major league baseball. I'll tell you about it sometime when we have a long ride ahead of us. We aren't far from Dave Barrett's parish. After canvassing the neighborhood, which, based on what we've seen and heard promises to be futile, thought we'd try to meet with his pastor."

"And hear about Barrett's sins?"

"That could expand and fine tune our list of leads. But since it can't happen, hope he'll be able to give us the name of Barrett's AA sponsor."

Pete scheduled an appointment with Dave Barrett's pastor ... and his, while Martin learned Cameron Remer was bailed out last night and appeared at the appointed

23

hour for his arraignment. He got Remer's address and contact information.

"Father Spicer won't be available until 12:30, and it's now 10:45," Martin said, glancing at his watch. "If we're correct about Barrett's neighbors, we'll finish canvassing the neighborhood in about ten minutes. So, since you live about ten minutes from here, we could grab lunch at your house and get back to the rectory in time for our meeting. It would be a time saver, because it would take less time to drive to your house, eat, and spend a little time with Katie and Teddy than it would take to drive to and from a restaurant, place an order, wait for our food, eat, and pay the bill."

"To say nothing about the time it takes to calculate the tip." Pete smiled.

Martin laughed and raised an eyebrow questioningly.

Martin didn't mention it, but Pete knew his partner continued his efforts to help Pete find segments of time with his baby, Teddy, who was now six months old. These efforts weren't purely altruistic. Martin had an ulterior motive. He wanted to prove that Pete could successfully combine fatherhood with the demands of their job.

Pete called home, and Katie was delighted with the idea of him and Martin coming for lunch.

They checked on the neighbors. Neither Pete nor Martin was surprised when they went zero for eight. They added return visits to their to do lists.

Pete called Katie to let her know they were on their way.

She, Teddy, and their dog Benji, greeted Pete and Martin at the front door.

The moment he saw his daddy, Teddy smiled, squealed, and reached for Pete, while Benji jumped up and down and licked Pete's hand, then Martin's.

Katie had set up a smorgasbord on the kitchen counter, consisting of meats, cheeses, Romaine and iceberg lettuce, carrots, celery, cauliflower, broccoli, apples, oranges, apricots, and grapes.

"Imagine what she could have done had we given her more than ten minutes." Martin chuckled. "The only thing missing is the martinis."

"Straight up or on the rocks?" Katie deadpanned. She could give as well as she received.

"Thanks, but it's a little early for me. How about a Diet Coke with a lime twist?"

"Admit it, Martin. It'll still be too early for you when you crawl into bed tonight," Pete said.

"Yeah, but don't tell the guys. I have a reputation to maintain."

Pete laughed and launched into an old hit written and recorded by Jimmy Dean, "'*Ev'ry mornin' at the mine you could see him arrive. He stood six foot six and weighed 245. Kinda broad at the shoulder and narrow at the hip, and everybody knew, ya didn't give no lip to Big Martin.*' Sorry, Martin. We need to change your name to something that's one syllable. It'll flow better."

"Haven't heard that one in about a hundred years," Martin said. "My grandpa loved it. I can't believe you remember the words."

"My mind is like a steel trap. A little rusty, but ..."

While eating, Pete held and played with Teddy. Martin played with Benji and snuck him a few morsels, so he didn't feel neglected, and Katie used the opportunity to run an errand.

"Speaking of nicknames," Martin said, "you can now call Teddy the King of Drool."

"Yeah. Holding him up over my head is now a bad idea. Whenever I forget and do that, more likely than not I end up with a face full of goo. But teething is much harder on him than it is on Katie and me."

"I told you he now sleeps through the night, didn't I?"

Martin smiled, nodded, and thought, *At least a half dozen times.* He loved the fact Pete was so enthralled with fatherhood.

Undeterred, Pete added, "He goes to bed at 7:00 and wakes up around 5:00, demanding a clean diaper. His wake up schedule fits well with mine. Bedtime much less so."

"Wait 'til you see this," Pete said, setting Teddy on the floor. Smiling proudly, he said, "Can you believe he now sits unsupported? Before you know it, he'll be reading bedtime stories to me."

"Yeah, but can he roll over and play dead?"

"He's halfway there. He rolls over—both ways. It took him awhile to conquer the stomach-to-back move. He hated when he moved from his back to his stomach, then had to stay that way for any time at all, staring at the floor."

"You could have solved that by getting more colorful floor coverings. Think about that before Teddy's brother or sister arrives. He'll have one or the other, won't he?"

"Heaven only knows, Martin."

"Knowing you the way I do, I doubt that."

Too quickly for Pete, he and Martin had to leave for their appointment at the rectory. It proved even more informative than they'd anticipated.

FIVE

Father Spicer

It surprised Pete when Father Spicer answered the door. He knew the priest and had often spoken with him, but never at the rectory. When he was a kid, all the rectories had a housekeeper who often seconded as the cook.

Father Spicer invited the two men in, led them to a sitting room, and offered them coffee or tea. Both declined, but Father fixed himself a mug of tea from a kettle on a hotplate.

The furniture in the room looked too ancient for a rectory that was probably less than a quarter of its age.

Antiques? Pete wondered. *Donated by a parishioner? Or is this a reflection of Father Spicer's taste?*

"We haven't spoken in a while," Father Spicer told Pete. "I hope all is well with Katie and Teddy. To what do I owe the honor?"

Pete explained they needed his help in investigating the murder of one of his parishioners or former parishioners.

"Murder?" Father Spicer gasped. "Which parishioner?"

"David Barrett," Pete said.

Father Spicer shook his head and said, "Just when he'd gotten his life back on track. I know you're a

27

detective, Pete, but I never thought you'd approach me in that capacity. How can I help?"

"We currently have little to go on," Pete said. "Spoke with both of his brothers, and now we're looking for a list of his friends ... and enemies. Heard he joined AA and wondering if his group is connected with your church?"

"We have a group, but I don't have a list of the members. Hate to be a stumbling block, but even if I could find one, not sure I'm allowed to share it."

"Believe me, Father, I understand," Pete said. "We don't want you to violate the members' right to privacy. Do you have a way of finding out the name of Dave's sponsor? If so, I'd like you to contact him and ask him to call me. He could be a valuable source of information about Dave's current problems, including people who may have wanted to hurt him. That information would help us with our investigation, Father."

"And if I get the name, but that person refuses to contact you?"

"At least you tried and we tried, and we'll keep looking."

"How well did you know Dave, Father?" Martin asked.

"Well enough to like and respect him, and he was always there when we needed someone to help us problem solve."

"If you don't mind my asking," Martin said, "with what kinds of problems?"

"Financial ones. When donations no longer covered everything, he helped us figure out where to cut and how much. He also gave us an additional, sizable donation." Father Spicer shook his head and said, "He'll be missed."

"Do you know if he was close to any of your parishioners?" Pete asked.

"He was always friendly, greeting everyone and asking about them and their families; but after Melissa died, he always came and left alone."

"Was anyone hurt by the budget cuts he helped you implement?" Pete asked.

"Unfortunately, yes. Almost everyone had to take a reduction in salary. It was that or eliminate some positions. Everyone, or almost everyone, voted in favor of salary reductions."

"Even so, that had to hurt them, and some more than others," Martin said.

"Yes, that's a given. One person found a new job and left. Another kept their job and got a part time job to compensate. But *neither* would take it out on David."

"Were the cuts anticipated to be permanent or temporary?" Martin asked.

"Permanent, but we continue hoping that won't be necessary."

"When were these cuts implemented?" Pete asked.

"A month ago."

"For us," Pete said, "there's about a ten-day delay between the end of the pay period and the issuance of checks. Is that true for your staff as well?"

After staring into space for a few seconds while he did the calculation, Father Spicer nodded.

"So the last check they received was the first one reflecting the reductions?" Pete asked.

"Yes."

"When is your staff paid?" Pete asked. "Twice a month, biweekly, or?"

"Biweekly, and to save you having to ask, they were paid last Friday." Father Spicer frowned. "And you're thinking that paycheck drove home the impact of the salary reductions, motivating a member of our staff to eliminate the person instrumental in their adoption. Relying on a trite cliché, 'You're barking up the wrong tree.' We wouldn't employ anyone placing so little value on a human life; and if you examined the salaries, you'd see money can't be a major motivator for them."

Both investigators wondered, but neither asked which employee quit and which one got a second job. There were other ways to get those answers. Better ways than putting Father Spicer further on the defensive.

Back in Martin's unmarked car, he told Pete, "Money is tight for lots of us these days. You don't suppose ..."

SIX

The List Grows

Shocked! That's how Joel Milroy looked and felt when Jack shared the news about his brother Dave's murder.

Without waiting for a response nor allowing for questions, Jack rushed out of Joel's office, nearly bowling over his legal assistant.

Joel spent several minutes, staring into space. Finally, he forced himself to return to the things he should have been doing while waiting for Dave Barrett to show at the courthouse this morning. Immersed in wrapping up a letter in time to get it postmarked today, he contemplated ignoring his ringing cellphone.

On the third ring, he grunted, grabbed the phone off his desk, and said, "Milroy Law Office."

Years ago, he'd contemplated finding someone to write a jingle, designed to attract clients. His wife suggested he use, "*It's the real thing.*" He'd explained he'd lose his shirt ... and their house, if Coca Cola decided to sue him for copyright infringement. "Or maybe they'd pay you for the advertising," she'd laughed.

As soon as Martin identified himself, but before he could ask any questions, Milroy asked, "Dave was murdered?"

"Yes, and I'm confident you're aware that at this time I can't share any details."

"I realize that, but there's nothing stopping me from talking. I know some things that might help you."

"Hang on, Joel. Let me put you on speaker, so my partner can hear you too." A moment later, Martin said, "Okay, Pete Culnane is on with us. What kind of information?"

"Cameron Remer arrived at the courthouse this morning at the eleventh hour. He looked like he'd spent the night in jail. He didn't. You probably already know that. Anyway, per my calculations, he could have murdered Dave and arrived at the courthouse by the time he dashed into the courtroom ... out of breath. I hope that's useful."

"In this business," Martin said, "there's no such thing as too much information, and we have some questions."

"Such as?"

"You spoke with Dave Barrett last night?"

"Yes. He called and asked me to be at the courthouse prior to his arraignment."

"And you discussed the reason he was arrested?"

"Briefly. He was tired, and we planned to talk this morning."

"Were you under the impression he was afraid of Cameron Remer?" Martin asked.

"I don't know if he was afraid of him, but he said he didn't think Remer was finished with him. Dave said Remer was angry that the police broke up the fight."

"Were you and David Barrett friends?" Martin asked.

"Not really. I mean, we didn't get together socially. I saw him and we spoke only when he had a legal issue."

"Was that frequent," Martin asked, "and was anything pending?"

"It was infrequent, and there was nothing pending."

"In that case," Martin asked, "am I correct in concluding you didn't see enough of him, or speak with him enough, to know if he was nervous or anxious about anything?"

"Well, of course he was nervous about the arraignment. He said Remer started the fight, and he only defended himself. He planned to plead innocent and was concerned doing that might irritate the judge. That's why he wanted me there ... just in case there was the unusual opportunity to say something in addition to entering his plea."

"Where was the fight?" Martin asked.

"In the Robert Street parking ramp. Remer attacked him at the end of the day, as he got out of the elevator to walk to his car."

"Had you represented him previously?" Martin asked.

"Once, when he was subpoenaed to testify as a witness to an armed robbery."

"If he was a witness, why did he need an attorney?" Martin asked.

"Because the accused threatened him and his wife. He asked for my help in negotiating with the police for protection before he testified and until the man, if convicted, was imprisoned. If he wasn't convicted and imprisoned, Dave wanted guarantees that he and his wife would be put into a witness protection program. Guarantees that would stand up to challenges."

"A witness protection program?" Pete asked. "Neither St. Paul nor Ramsey County has a witness protection program. That would only have been possible if the accused was brought up on federal charges."

"Correct, and this information isn't for public consumption." Joel lowered his voice and continued, "The case had to do with the attack of an elderly woman. She was from one of the moneyed families in St. Paul. Her family said she was a bit eccentric and loved to exercise her independence by going downtown alone, shopping, and roving around in the skyways. Concerned about her physical and emotional well-being if her attacker wasn't prosecuted, her family offered to find a place for Dave and his wife and cover all costs."

"How long ago was all this?" Martin asked.

"About a decade ago. I'd just graduated from law school, and it was one of my first cases. I was pumped that Dave put so much confidence in me and resolved to not let him regret it."

"Where did this armed robbery occur?" Pete asked.

"In the Golden Rule Building. Dave was on the way up the stairs to his office on the mezzanine level and heard a woman scream. He ran the rest of the way up the stairs and toward the screams. The robber saw him coming, hit the woman over the head with his gun, yanked her purse out of her hands, and took off. Dave stopped to check on the woman, then chased him. By then, the guy had escaped or found a place to hide. Dave didn't find him, but he returned to the woman, called 911, and stayed with her until the paramedics arrived."

"Was the robber apprehended, convicted, and imprisoned?" Pete asked.

"Yes to all those things, but I think he was recently paroled."

"Did Dave mention the man being paroled when you spoke last night?" Martin asked.

"No, but I doubt he knew. I didn't find out about it until this morning."

34

"What is the man's name?" Martin asked.

"Edgar Waltham."

"Where was the trial?" Pete asked.

"Ramsey County."

"Do you know where he was imprisoned?" Pete asked.

"Yes. Stillwater."

"Anyone or anything else?" Martin asked. He refused to jump to conclusions, but that didn't reduce his determination to contact the Minnesota Department of Corrections ASAP to get Waltham's release date and the name and contact information for his probation officer.

"No," Joel said, "and I realize that neither Remer nor Waltham may have anything to do with what happened today."

Martin said, "We appreciate the information and we'll follow up on all of it. I don't want to raise your anxiety level, Joel, but would Waltham remember you and credit you as being instrumental in his conviction?"

"Not sure how he'd have heard my name, since I wasn't part of the prosecutorial team. Just the same, thanks. I'll keep my guard up."

Pete bit his lip. He knew Waltham's attorney may have told him the name of the attorney who'd jumped through so many hoops to protect the witness ... the person who may have sealed Waltham's conviction and ten years in prison.

SEVEN
Gathering Information

As Martin disconnected from his call to Joel Milroy, Pete said, "Way to go, Martin!"

"Thanks, Pete." Martin smiled, pleased with the compliment. "Unless you have something else in mind," he added, "I'll contact the Minnesota Department of Corrections to get the info about Waltham."

"You're on a roll. I won't get in your way. I tried and failed to reach Cameron Remer. So while you do that, I'll work on the contact information for Barrett's best man, Mike Hinckley. Because the incident with Waltham occurred in the Golden Rule Building, let's also prioritize speaking with people working there. Dave might have made a name for himself that day and, unless there's a large turnover, some of the people working there should know him and might have noticed if something peculiar has been happening in the vicinity of his office."

Pete started with a people search for a Michael Hinckley living anywhere in Maryland. Unfortunately, there were half a dozen. At least his name wasn't Michael Hinkle. That name had three times as many matches. Calling the six listed phone numbers until someone answered, hoping one of them was the man they sought, could be a failed effort and a major waste of time.

It might have helped to know Michael's middle name. Father Spicer might have it in his records from

Dave's wedding, but Pete worried that he and Martin had already pushed the priest too far. And he didn't want to risk being assigned a penance of praying all four mysteries of the rosary the next time he went to confession. He smiled at the uproar a penance like that would create, once word got out. And it would get out.

Pete grew up with three mysteries of the rosary, the Joyful, Sorrowful, and Glorious. Then, in 2002, the pope, St. John Paul II, added the Luminous. Pete still couldn't rattle those mysteries off the way he could the ones he grew up with.

He decided to return to a resource he relied upon in the first case he and Martin worked together. He called the alumni office at Macalester College, the college Dave Barrett and Mike Hinckley attended. The last time Pete contacted that office, he needed to reach Megan Alden, the sister of a homeless man whose body was found on St. Paul's upper landing.

Pete hoped Mike Hinckley was a contributor, attended college functions, subscribed to the newsletter, or for some other reason made his way onto their mailing lists or database.

After explaining that Megan no longer worked there, the current director of alumni relations did a search and found a Michael Robert Hinckley who graduated in 1999. *That was twenty years ago and would make him about forty-two*, Pete thought. He knew David Barrett was forty-two.

At Pete's request, she also looked for a David Barrett in their listings. A minute later, she said, "A David Dennis Barrett also graduated in 1999."

Reluctantly, she provided Mike's address and phone numbers, doing so only after calling the central number for headquarters, getting Pete's number from them, and calling him back. In spite of all that, he knew it was far faster than resorting to the numbers provided by the people finder on the internet.

Concluding his call, Martin said, "I reached Corrections. Joel was right. Edgar Waltham was paroled ten days ago. So I called his probation officer. Waltham attended the first meeting, the one mandated to occur within seventy-two hours of his release. They scheduled the next meeting for a month later, on October 10. That's three weeks from tomorrow."

"According to his probation officer, Waltham was uptight at the initial meeting but he said everything was fine. He claimed to have several upcoming job interviews and said he was certain he'll get at least one offer. But he couldn't remember any of the company names, and he hadn't thought to bring the list. Said he's saving money by living with a widowed sister until he gets a job. His sister's a good cook, so he's saving money there too. He makes up for the room and board by helping her fix the things that are forever breaking. He loves the privacy."

"At their first meeting, the probation officer had no basis for requiring they meet more than monthly. He's waiting to see how long that lasts. By the way, I got Waltham's address and phone number." Martin smiled.

Pete gave him a thumbs up.

Before leaving for the Golden Rule Building, they printed several copies of Cameron Remer's driver's license photo and Edgar Waltham's prison photo, cropping the second photo to prevent his wardrobe from biasing perceptions.

On their way downtown, Pete said, "Do you know how the Golden Rule Building got its name?"

"Because anyone wanting to rent office space had to swear they'd obey the golden rule in all of their dealings, treating everyone the way they wanted to be treated?"

"Martin, you are so close ... but couldn't be more wrong. Back in 1888 the Golden Rule opened a department store at that location. Donaldson's later bought the Golden Rule, and that store became Donaldson's Golden Rule. Eventually, it became simply Donaldson's."

"Are you handing me a line?"

"No, I'm trying to insure that you pass the history test the next time you try for a promotion."

"I'd never do that, Pete. You couldn't function without me. Seriously, how did you know about the Golden Rule Department Store?"

"Grandma Jackie told me. She said Donaldson's and Dayton's used to draw her downtown on a regular basis. I'll never forget the times she took me to lunch at Dayton's Department Store. As a young kid, I always felt awestruck by all the downtown traffic and commotion. The last time we went was shortly before they closed the store. By then, it had gone from Dayton's to Marshall Fields to Macy's. I don't know who regretted the final closing six years ago more, Grandma Jackie or me."

After parking on 7th Place, Pete and Martin walked to the Golden Rule Building and climbed the grand, expansive stairway to the mezzanine. Knowing Dave Barrett ran up these stairs to stop Edgar Waltham, they looked around when reaching the mezzanine,, wondering where in the expansive area the attack occurred.

Next they did a quick tour of the mezzanine, getting a feel for the types of businesses located there. They saw the Minnesota Department of Health's Center for Health Statistics, an Army recruiting office, the building manager's office, a coffee shop, Barrett Accounting, and Capital Street Financial Services.

Rather than starting with the offices closest to the open area at the top of the stairs, they began with the places with the clearest views of the mezzanine. That included Capital Street, the building manager, and the coffee shop.

First they went to the coffee shop, since it seemed to have the most traffic ... and Diet Coke. After identifying themselves, they asked the cashier, who doubled as the hostess, how long she'd worked there. Based on her estimated age, they weren't optimistic.

Turned out she began two years ago, but that didn't mean she had to be excluded. Martin pulled out a copy of Edgar Waltham's photo and asked if he was a regular customer.

"Looks familiar, but I can't be sure." She frowned. "Want me to ask Beth? She's here five days a week and knows most of our regulars by name. What's his name?"

"How about if we talk to Beth and see if she recognizes him before I say?" Martin asked.

She rolled her eyes, gave him a whatever look and returned a long minute later with a woman who looked like she might have shopped at the original Golden Rule Department Store.

Again, Pete and Martin identified themselves. Then Pete began by asking if she worked the day a decade or so ago when a woman was attacked by a man on the mezzanine level, and another man chased him away.

"Which time are you referring to, Sweetie?" she asked. "Downtown is deteriorating. It isn't nearly as safe as it used to be. Back when I started working downtown, I never worried about walking alone to and from my job. Not even after dark. Not so much anymore."

"The time I'm talking about happened about ten years ago," Pete said. "A guy named Dave Barrett ran the attacker off. Do you know Dave?"

"Oh, that time. Yes, I remember it, and I know Dave. He became quite the hero after that happened. He's quiet, but he'd give you the shirt off his back. He's my biggest tipper," she said and smiled.

"Did you see the man he chased off?" Martin asked.

"I got a look at him and called 911, in case Dave needed help. I was on my way to the airport. Had to catch a flight to help my mom, so I couldn't hang around. Hurried off, afraid of missing my bus ... and my flight. I ended up staying with Mom for almost a year. Never thought about it again."

Martin showed her the photo of Waltham and asked if he might have been the attacker.

Beth glanced at the photo, shook her head and said, "Not a chance. The one thing I remember about the guy is he had a rose-colored birthmark on his," she put a hand up and touched one of her cheeks, then the other and said, "on his right cheek."

"Did you mention the birthmark when you called 911?" Martin asked.

Both he and Pete wondered, *How could a detail as significant as that be overlooked in the arrest and conviction?*

"I must have, but I was so rattled and nervous about missing my flight, I'm not positive."

"Where were you when you saw the birthmark?" Pete asked.

"About where we're standing right now," Beth said.

"Would someone coming up the stairs and running toward that man have seen him from the same angle?" Pete asked, thinking out loud.

Beth walked out of the coffee shop and toward the stairs. About halfway there, she stopped and said, "It happened right about here, and the guy had his back to the stairs. That's why I saw the right side of his face. Unless he turned his body or his head, I don't think anyone coming up the stairs or running from that direction could have seen the right side of his face. I'm not sure they'd have seen his face at all, but even if he turned, they'd probably have seen the left side, not the right. Why?"

"Actually, it has nothing to do with the case we're working. Just surprised to hear about the birthmark. Also curious about whether the victim would have seen it?"

"I doubt it. I didn't see him approach her, but when I saw them, he was behind her with one hand over her mouth and the other holding the gun. With an identifying characteristic like that birthmark, I would think he attacked her from behind and didn't let her see his face."

Pete pulled out the photo of Waltham and asked, "How about the man in this photo? Have you seen him around here?"

"I've only seen him recently, like in the last week or so, wandering around here, on the mezzanine, I mean, and in the skyway."

"When did you last see him?" Pete asked.

Beth brought an index finger to her lips and furrowed her brow. After several seconds, she said, "Monday. I know it was Monday, because that was the day a young girl jumped out of her seat in the coffee shop and knocked me down. Her mother helped me up while yelling at her. The girl started crying. She looked so much like one of my granddaughters. I bent down, looked her straight in the eye and told her it happens all the time, and it wasn't her fault. Then I treated her to a strawberry sundae. I wanted to help her feel better. Her mom wanted to pay for it. No way."

"Anyway," Beth continued, "that guy must have spent at least an hour in the mezzanine. It seemed every time I waited on a booth, I saw him. He looked like he was expecting someone. I have no idea whether that person ever showed or he just gave up and left."

"You can see Dave Barrett's office from here, right?" Pete asked.

"Yes, dear, my vision isn't that bad." Beth chuckled.

"Did he seem to take any special interest in Dave's office?" Pete asked.

"Might have. He certainly spent a lot of time in that area. Why are you asking all these questions?"

"We're looking for the man in that photo," Pete said, and we greatly appreciate your help. Got a minute to get us a couple of Diet Cokes we can take with us?"

"You bet, Sweetie!"

Beth returned with two cans of Diet Coke and two Styrofoam cups filled with ice.

Pete paid her and included a tip that dwarfed the size of Dave's tips. He wasn't competing with Dave. He was grateful for her assistance.

Their next stop was at the building manager's office. When they walked in, they saw him sitting at a desk, staring at the computer monitor. He didn't look up until Martin cleared his throat. So the outlook wasn't promising.

When they showed him their badges and IDs, wide-eyed, he gasped, "Was there another attack in the building?"

"We're here about an attack that occurred more than a decade ago," Pete said.

"Thank goodness," he sighed.

Ever the optimist, Martin asked how long he'd been the building manager and officed in this space.

"Twelve years, and it's getting harder and harder to rent vacant space."

He remembered the attack on the mezzanine about ten years ago, but had only heard about it. He said David Barrett is a wonderful tenant. He always pays his rent in advance, and he never creates a ruckus or a mess. He didn't recognize Waltham, and he hadn't noticed him recently in the Golden Rule ... nor anywhere else.

The receptionist at Capital Street greeted the two investigators, asked how she could help, and offered them a beverage. The name plaque on her desk identified her as Lynn Preston.

Since they'd just finished their Cokes, they turned down her offer and asked to speak with someone who worked there eleven years ago.

"Only one of our staff goes back that far," she said. "He's on the phone, but should be available shortly. May I have your names?"

When Pete and Martin produced their IDs, she said, "Oh, do you want me to ask him to hang up and come right out?"

Pete smiled and said, "We're happy to wait, if it will only be a few minutes."

A short time later, a smiling middle-aged man entered the reception area, hand extended. He introduced himself as Phillip Lindstrom.

While following Lindstrom to the office at the end of the hallway, one thing became clear. If he was in his office, unless someone alerted him, Lindstrom wasn't

44

likely to become aware of the happenings outside Capital Street's door. However, he had to get to and from their offices, and that could happen multiple times each day.

Handing Lindstrom the photo of Edgar Waltham, Martin asked if the man in the photo looked familiar.

"He looks much worse for the wear," Lindstrom said, "but isn't he the man convicted of an armed robbery in this building more than a decade ago?"

"You helped take him down?" Martin asked, without narrowing down the plethora of ways that statement could be interpreted.

"If you're asking if I helped in his capture or prosecution, the answer is no. Because my company offices were located so close to the scene of the crime, I read every article written about it in both the St. Paul and Minneapolis newspapers, and I studied and made copies of the photos of him. If he was freed, which in my opinion happens far too often, no offense intended, I wanted to make sure my staff and I recognized him, steered clear of him, and called 911 at the slightest provocation."

"Put yourself in my position," Lindstrom continued. "I have a staff of twenty. All of them are like my children ... even those too old for that to be biologically feasible. When that woman was attacked, my concern for the safety of my staff escalated. Ever since, when the time comes to renew my lease, I reexamine the issue. And it isn't just this building. It's downtown St. Paul."

"Why do you stay here?" Pete asked.

Lindstrom threaded his fingers together on his desktop and said, "Loyalty. We've been here for more than twenty years."

"Have you seen the face in that photo recently, either in this building or anywhere?" Martin asked.

"Isn't he in prison?"

"Not anymore," Martin said. "He completed his sentence and was paroled."

Lindstrom threw up his hands and shook his head.

"We'd like to speak with your staff," Pete said.

"Okay, I'll have them report to the large meeting room."

"We prefer meeting with them individually," Pete said.

"Fine. Follow me. I'll take you to the small meeting room and send them in one by one. Anything else?"

"Thanks. That should do it, at least for now," Pete said.

He and Martin spent almost an hour meeting with the Capital Street employees. No one recognized ... or at least admitted to recognizing Waltham. Nor did they remember ... or admit to remembering seeing him in the Golden Rule Building, downtown, or anywhere else.

EIGHT

Edgar Waltham's Sister, Elaine

Reaching Martin's unmarked car, Pete again called Cameron Remer's cellphone. He was disappointed but not surprised when it proved as futile as the last time. "Remer lives in Lake Elmo and Waltham lives in an apartment on West Minnehaha, near Grotto," he said. "How about starting with Waltham and working our way east, Martin?"

"Because we'll finish with either Remer or Waltham at dinnertime, and you like the food better in or near Lake Elmo?"

"Of course not. The patio at the Lakewood Tavern is the drawing card." Pete chuckled.

"Do you think they're unaware of our calls or are they ignoring them?" Martin asked.

Pete smiled and asked, "Or maybe because the caller ID doesn't identify us? But who would risk missing a spam call from Brazil, India, Nigeria, or China, for instance, and forgo the opportunity to broaden their global perspective?"

"My family members, for starters." Martin grinned.

"And for that reason, we won't permit our unanswered calls to dissuade us. We'll drop in, hoping they're better at answering the door than the phone."

Waltham lived with his sister in one of nine appealing, three-story, brown brick and beige stucco apartment buildings. The complex was tucked in a neighborhood of homes constructed in the 1920s through the 1940s. They ran the gamut in both design and the level of upkeep. Either the trees in the neighborhood survived Dutch elm disease or their replacements spent the ensuing years growing to the point where they now shaded the street, providing a beautiful, cozy aura.

The name plaque over Edgar Waltham's sister's mailbox said, "Elaine Waltham."

Never married, went back to her maiden name, or never used her husband's last name? Pete wondered. *Why did she take in her brother after he was paroled?*

Ascending two flights of stairs and reaching the apartment Edgar Waltham currently called his domicile, Martin positioned himself to the left of the door, while Pete stood to the right. A bit too cautious? Was there such a thing?

Martin reached over and knocked loud enough to be heard at the far end of the apartment.

Both men heard a feminine sounding voice call out, "Coming."

Next came the sounds of shuffling papers and crackling bags, bags like those commonly used for some kind of chips or popcorn. That was followed by the sound of cupboard doors in need of felt protectors closing a bit too hard. Finally, Pete and Martin heard the same voice coming from the other side of the door asking, "Who is it?"

"St. Paul police," Pete said. "We have a few questions."

"Why me? Or is this about my brother?"

"Open the door and we'll be happy to discuss it," Pete said.

They heard the clunk of a deadbolt, before she opened the door just enough to get a glimpse at them, and permit them to see one of her eyes, her nose, and a bit of her mouth. The chain, which remained in place, limited the size of the opening ... but only if no one gave the door a swift kick or lunged at it.

"Before I let you in, let me see your badges and IDs," she said.

Accommodating her, Pete and Martin held both up to the opening.

Then without a word, the door closed, they heard the sound of the chain, and the door opened slowly. In front of them stood a slim, middle-aged woman of average height, with carefully styled, gray-streaked, dark-brown hair, greenish-blue eyes, and a slightly upturned nose. She wore blue jeans and a flowered, short-sleeved top.

With one hand on the door and the other on her hip, she said, "Okay, let's hear it. Why are you here?"

"May we come in?" Pete asked.

She rolled her eyes, said, "Okay," stepped back, and waved them in.

The door opened into her living room, and the kitchen and dining area lay just to the left. The table was empty and looked clean, as did the countertops and carpet. The tables in the living room were stacked with newspapers, magazines, and books.

Barely inside the door, with the play-by-play broadcast of the Twins versus White Sox game in the background, Pete asked, "You're Ms. Waltham?"

"Yes, and why are you here?"

"We'd like to speak with you and your brother." Pete said.

"Well, Edgar isn't here."

Might be just as well, Pete thought. *We might get more out of her when he isn't around.* "In that case," he said, "mind if we ask a few questions?"

"First, have a seat," she said, motioning to the living room. Then she picked up the remote that sat on the coffee table and turned off the Twins game, saying, "It keeps me company."

The living room held a couch with a floral pattern, two oversized forest-green chairs, a coffee table, and an end table. A large, flat-screened TV hung on the wall, across from the couch.

"Your questions are about?" she asked.

"We understand your brother lives with you," Martin said.

"Yes. Despite a good job market, he's having a difficult time. I imagine you know he was a paramedic. I'm furious that his unjust record as a felon makes his return to that line of work impossible. It may make sense … in some cases, but not for someone who was falsely convicted. Right now, life seems so unfair. I fear very soon he'll be forced to accept a job as a taxi driver, a deliveryman—if they'll take someone with a record, a sanitation engineer, or who knows what?" She frowned. "It's heartbreaking, because he was framed."

With that last statement, Elaine watched for a reaction from Pete, Martin, or both, hoping. Based on their expressions, you'd think she'd just said something as astonishing as, "The sky is blue on cloud-free days."

So she continued, "He had a conceal and carry permit and had every right to be carrying that gun. The gun and his presence in the skyway, in a different building than the crime, were the reasons he was arrested … and convicted."

"Didn't someone identify him?" Martin asked.

"How can anyone identify a guy who was a building away and hadn't set foot in the Golden Rule Building that day? When arrested, Ed wore khakis, a black sweatshirt, and a baseball cap. Maybe the guy who attacked the woman was dressed similarly. Besides, you know, and I know, how unreliable eyewitnesses can be. Did the eyewitness get a good look at the attacker's face? Ed said he never set eyes on him before the trial. If the eyewitness didn't get a *good* look at the attacker, how did he know it was Ed?"

Sounds like she should have been Ed's defense attorney, Pete thought.

"Frankly," she continued, "all of this hasn't done much for my opinion of law enforcement or the judicial system. A friend told me the police care most about the percentage of crimes solved. Getting the right person convicted runs a distant second. Based on what happened to Ed, it seems she was right." Elaine scowled at Pete and Martin.

After a long pause, which she spent staring at her hands, Elaine looked each man straight in the eye. "Ed would be furious if he knew I told you," she said. "I'm going to anyway. It gives you an accurate picture of the man I know. However, please never tell him I told you." She shook an index finger at them.

"He had no alibi, and the trial wasn't going well, so I came up with a solution. I told Ed I'd perjure myself, claiming he and I were together that afternoon. He almost went crazy. He forbade me from doing that. He said lying, especially under oath, was never the answer. He suggested I try praying. Well, it wasn't like I hadn't already been doing that."

"I didn't miss a minute of his trial. After the opening statements, I told Ed he had to find a different attorney. You should have seen the guy he hired. He was frumpy, and he could have put a jury of five-year-olds on a sugar-and-caffeine high to sleep. If the trial consisted only of opening statements, I'd probably have voted to convict Ed. Seriously, his attorney was pathetic." Elaine shook her head forlornly.

"How did he find his attorney?" Martin asked.

"Ed was newly divorced, so money was tight. He wanted nothing more to do with his divorce attorney, so he asked a couple of friends for referrals. The attorney he went with was someone's brother-in-law. That made me nervous, and I told him he couldn't risk it. He needed to get the best of the best. I said I'd use some of the money in my retirement account. He wouldn't hear of it. He said he was innocent and only needed someone to go through the process for him. I told him that was a mighty big gamble. I had no idea just how big."

Elaine blew out a long breath and continued, "Ed is the one who filed for the divorce, and his ex still hates him for it. The prosecution had her testify against him. She lied through her teeth. I saw Ed pass all kinds of notes to his attorney during her testimony. His attorney ignored every single one of them."

Running her fingers through her hair, Elaine added, "They got divorced after Ed found her in bed with her boyfriend. He'd switched shifts with a friend and came home when she expected him to be working. Even so, she got the kids, the house, half of their savings, and Ed's retirement. Ed got the car and the other half of their savings and his retirement."

"As it turned out," she continued, "it would have been well worth whatever it cost for a good attorney. But, how could we know what lay ahead?"

"I'm fifteen years older than Ed. I'm more like a second mother than his sister. I've known him his entire life. I know he'd never hurt a woman, much less attempt to steal her purse. Not even if he was starving! The whole prison sentence and now his inability to return to work in his chosen profession, the field he loves, make me sick. I wish I knew how to help." She moaned.

Pete asked, "Did you testify at his trial?"

"Yes, and I said what I just told you. He'd never do what they accused him of. The prosecution said my testimony was equivalent to having a spouse testify, and my opinion was too biased to hold any weight."

"Any idea when Edgar will return?" Martin asked.

Looking at her watch, Elaine said, "It's 4:30. He usually gets back between 5:30 and 6:00, and we always eat at 6:30."

"What time does his day usually begin?" Martin asked.

"He's always out the door at 7:50 due to the bus schedule."

Pete said. "We'll check back, just not sure when." *Or whether he'll disappear if he knows we're coming,* he thought and wondered, *If she was that incensed over Edgar's being accused and convicted of armed robbery, it doesn't take much of an imagination to picture how she'd react to his being suspected of murder.*

On their way back to the unmarked car and clear of the building, Martin said, "If her brother is innocent, he's already lost ten years of his life and is now having trouble finding a job. It would be understandable for them both to hate the eyewitness, as well as cops, attorneys, and the whole legal system."

"Yes," Pete sighed. "It's disconcerting to think Edgar may have been innocent."

"Yeah, it takes a lot of the satisfaction out of the job, doesn't it."

As he reached for the door handle, Pete felt his phone vibrate. *Remer? Elaine Waltham? Father Spicer?*

He pulled the phone out of his pocket, slid into the passenger side seat, and looked at the screen. He didn't recognize the number.

NINE
Clark Lonsdale, Dave's Sponsor

"**P**eter Culnane," he answered, waiting for a hangup or other sign the person dialed the wrong number.

Instead, the caller said, "This is Clark Lonsdale. Hank Spicer asked me to call you. Is this a good time?"

"I'm so glad you called, and your timing couldn't be better. Where are you? My partner and I would like to meet with you, and we're happy to come wherever you are."

After a protracted pause, Clark said, "I just got off work. Where are you?"

"We're in the Frogtown neighborhood. How about you?"

"I work in an office building located near United Hospital. We could meet at Cossetta's. It's too early for dinner, but we could get something to drink."

"That works, we can be there in about ten minutes."

"Okay. I'm wearing aqua surgical scrubs. Could be a lot of people dressed similarly, so look for someone with black hair in need of a trim and square glasses with navy frames. That should narrow it down. I'll wait for you near the side door. See you soon."

After disconnecting, Pete checked to see who'd called while he spoke with Lonsdale. It was Don from the ME's office. In a hurry to learn the reason for that call, he called Don, without checking for a message.

Don answered, saying, "Does this mean you're unhappy about it and want us to find a way?"

"You've lost me," Pete said.

"I take it you didn't listen to my voicemail." Don laughed.

"No. Guess that was a mistake, huh? I was in a hurry."

"How unusual, Pete. The reason I called is to let you know we scheduled David Barrett's autopsy for first thing tomorrow morning. With a spike in opium deaths and the fatalities from the pileup on Highway 36 this morning, plus the usual load, we're backed up. So unless you'll be up in arms about that ..."

"Actually, Don, it should work well for me. As always, I want to be there, and it would be hard pulling myself away from the interviews Martin and I have planned for today. What time?"

"Since we do our best to schedule all of them within twenty-four hours, and we're doing our best to catch up, we scheduled it for 7:00."

"See you then," Pete said and tucked away his phone.

Martin glanced at him and asked, "Well?"

"The autopsy is scheduled for 7:00 a.m. tomorrow. So I'll be tied up until around 9:00 or 10:00, and possibly as late as 11:00. Why don't you relax a bit and report in at 9:00 or so?"

"Sold." Martin smiled. "And when I get in, I'll research our next contacts."

True to his word, Clark stood just inside the door, looking apprehensive. He appeared to be in his late forties or early fifties, and average height and build. In addition to the shaggy, black hair and blue eyeglasses he'd mentioned, Clark had big, blue eyes, a large nose, and full lips.

As soon as introductions were out of the way, he said, "If you're wondering about my garb, I'm a PA ... a physician's assistant." Then he blurted out, "What happened to Dave?"

"Hang on," Pete said. "I'm thirsty. Let's get something to drink." He turned and walked to the front of the cafeteria-style restaurant.

The three men placed their orders. Pete and Martin got their usual, Diet Coke, and Pete was pleased that Lonsdale stayed away from the few alcoholic options.

"Might have significantly more privacy in the unmarked car," Pete said. "What do you think, Clark?"

"Whatever you think," Clark said, and followed Pete out the side door to the parking lot.

Martin had parked on the far end of the lot, and the foot traffic was nearly nonexistent. So the men took advantage of what could be one of the last warm fall days. They lined up alongside the unmarked car and used it as a backrest, with Lonsdale in the middle.

"First," Pete said, "Dave's murder is an active investigation. We understand you hate being kept in the dark, but for now, that's all we can tell you. So let me back up. I assume Father Spicer told you that, respecting the anonymity AA provides, he wouldn't give us your name."

Lonsdale nodded and said, "I appreciate the fact he let me decide whether or not to meet with you. But why do you want to speak with me? Am I a suspect, because Dave and I got together last Sunday?"

"We didn't know about that meeting," Pete said. "Dave's brothers know little about his friends. We're looking for everyone who knew him and might be able to answer a few questions. For example, was anyone angry with him? Did anyone have a reason to seek revenge? Had he been concerned about or afraid of anyone? In the recent past, did he seem more nervous or anxious? Those sorts of things."

"First, I never noticed, nor was I aware of any of those things. The closest I can come is this. Dave and I spoke often. After the meetings, we usually found a place to talk. A guy hassled him a couple of times, telling Dave to stay away from his wife and stop flirting with her."

"Last Sunday, the guy and his wife were with another couple in the same restaurant as Dave and me. Their table was across the room. His wife spent an uncomfortable amount of time staring at Dave, and I thought it peculiar that she was so obvious about it."

"As best I could tell, Dave didn't pay any attention to her, and I don't think he was aware of her staring, because he neither reacted nor said anything. Had he known, I think he'd have done one or both. In fact, he would probably have made a joke about it."

"Suddenly," Clark continued, "her husband stood and started waving his arms and shouting. The noise level in the restaurant was too high for me to understand anything he said. Then he slammed his chair into the table and stomped over to Dave and me. He got in Dave's face, wagged his finger at Dave, and said, 'Try anything and I'll make you sorry you were born!' I think everyone in the place heard and understood every word. You see, when the commotion began, it got as quiet as a tomb in there." Clark's face reddened, and he said, "Sorry, poor choice of words."

Shaking it off, he continued, "A minute later, the maître d came over and escorted the guy, forcibly, back to his table. He, his wife, and the couple with them left a few minutes later."

"The guy was obviously drunk, and he knew Dave's name. Dave didn't seem concerned. In fact, when I said something, Dave just brushed it off."

"I asked how the guy knew his name, and he said they'd been friends ... until his wife died. Then he said he felt like a fifth wheel and always begged off."

"Did he tell you the guy's name?" Martin asked.

"He didn't have to. I don't know him, but I know his name."

"*Because of AA*? Pete wondered and asked, "His name is?"

"Gordon Shevlin."

"You knew his name," Pete said. "How about an address?"

"Only that it's somewhere south of downtown, such as West St. Paul, South St. Paul, or Mendota Heights."

"Anything else you can tell us to help narrow it down?" Pete asked.

Clark thought for a few seconds, then asked, "Would it help to know he works for the City of St. Paul ... in the Public Works Department?"

Pete nodded.

"You should know that I asked Dave if he thought the guy's wife might be attracted to him, and he said it didn't matter. If she was, it was a one-way street. It was obvious he didn't want to talk about it, so I didn't push."

"How do you read it, Clark?" Martin asked. "Was it the alcohol speaking? Is that why Shevlin acted the way he did?"

"Both Dave and I thought so."

"If they used to be friends, the guy would know not only his name, but also his address," Martin said.

"I know," Clark sighed. "I thought of him right away, when I heard someone murdered Dave."

TEN

Cameron and Kimberly Remer

"Lake Elmo or bust?" Martin asked as he and Pete buckled in, and he started the car.

"Yeah. I'm amazed I got you away from Cossetta's before you enjoyed a slice of pizza or a gelato ... or both." Pete laughed.

"It was tempting, but I'm still struggling to eat what people like you call sensibly, so I can keep off the pounds. There are days when I can't help wondering if it's worth it."

"Each time my resolve flags, Martin, I remember that thirty seconds after I eat something sensational, I may as well not have eaten it. The taste is gone. Unfortunately, the after effects, namely the pounds, are not."

"But Pete, you're thin as a rail, and you've never had a weight problem."

"Now that I'm approaching forty, I worry about love handles, and I'm determined not to let them win the battle."

"Katie might like you better that way, Pete."

"She loves me the way I am. She finds comfort in the familiar."

"Well, it's nice knowing I'm not the only one in this car who works to keep the pounds off." Martin smiled and gave himself an imaginary pat on the back.

"And I'm impressed by the way you've kept the pounds off, Martin. It's often harder than losing them in the first place."

On the way to Lake Elmo, which was about twenty minutes away, Pete again called Cameron Remer. The result was the same, and he didn't leave a message. If he did, it could give Remer a heads up that they were headed his way. Next he did a people search for a Gordon Shevlin living in Minnesota, before he resorted to contacting St. Paul Public Works. He smiled when there was only one, and he lived in South St. Paul.

Martin got on eastbound I-94 and followed it to the County Road 19 exit. Fortunately, he and Pete weren't addicted to shopping. Had they been, the plethora of options at the Shoppes at Arbor Lakes, which sat on the south side of this exit, might have been too much to resist. Instead, bent on solving this crime, they went north one block, then right on the frontage road, Hudson Boulevard North, left on Lake Elmo Avenue, right onto Fifth Street, and entered the Hunter's Crossing Community. By all indications, it was an upper middle class neighborhood. Pete glanced at the digital clock on the dashboard. It said 5:33, and he hoped Remer and his family didn't eat dinner this early.

Still in its infancy, this attractive community of two-story, craftsman style homes sported exterior colors tending toward earth tones, including several shades of gray, beige, and tan.

Trees in the front yards were the same age as the houses. But the size of the maples, birch trees, and pines in the back yards indicated they'd survived the construction of the community.

Martin parked two homes away, and he and Pete followed the sidewalk that existed only on Remer's side of the street. His slate-gray home had a triple garage. Walking up the driveway, both men noted the dark-gray pavers surrounding the bushes and trees. Up two steps stood the front door and a small porch with two white-painted wood rocking chairs.

Martin rang the doorbell, hoping. The sun wouldn't set for almost two hours, so they couldn't rely on interior lighting to indicate the presence or absence of the occupants.

Seconds later, the door opened wide, and a smiling woman looked out at them. With a little girl voice, she asked what she could do for them.

The as yet unidentified woman was pretty and in her early thirties. She had blonde hair styled to accentuate her small features and warm brown eyes. She was average height and looked like she stuck to an exercise regime. Her leggings and scoop-necked top left little to the imagination.

Pete and Martin produced their badges and IDs and asked her name. Research told them Mrs. Remer's first name was Kimberly, and that's the name she provided.

"Is Cameron home?" Pete asked.

"Yes. Is he in more trouble? He was arrested last night, but you must know that. Is that why you're here? I'm fed up with him." She blushed, put her hand over her mouth, and said, "*Please*, don't tell Cam I said anything. He'll go ballistic."

She invited them in. That meant they went three for three that afternoon. It was a record even Ty Cobb, Oscar Charleston, Rogers Hornsby, and Shoeless Joe Jackson would have admired.

"Follow me," she said, and led them past a small office on the right and the up and down stairways on the left. The open floor plan brought them into an area with the kitchen and dining area on the left and the family room with a large, brick fireplace on the right. The smell of fresh-baked chocolate chip cookies that met them when she opened the door intensified as they moved toward the kitchen.

How many sit-ups does it take to compensate for a chocolate chip cookie? Martin wondered.

It looked like someone had just completed a thorough cleaning. The chandelier in the entryway sparkled, the hardwood floors were dirt and dust free, the kitchen countertops held no clutter or dirty dishes.

Approaching the family room, Kimberly said, "Dear, these men would like to speak with you."

Startled, Cameron yelled, "What the hell!" as he snapped his book shut, swung his feet off the coffee table and jumped up from the couch.

Per his driver's license, Cameron Remer was thirty-two years old—ten years younger than Dave Barrett. He stood six feet tall and weighed two hundred pounds.

Based on his appearance, Pete thought, *he should have been able to make short work of Dave Barret, unless Dave was a pro at dodging punches.*

Cameron had dark-brown hair, bushy eyebrows, deep-set brown eyes, and a nose that looked like it had been broken at least once. His face bore no signs of yesterday's scuffle with Barrett. He wore tan chinos and a long-sleeved quarter-zip green shirt.

The two investigators noticed a glass with ice and brown liquid in a coaster on the end table alongside the couch. Both wondered if it was iced tea or something with more of a kick.

Glaring at Kimberly, Cameron growled, "What do they want this time of the day?"

Why ask her, not us? Pete and Martin wondered.

"Just a few minutes of your time," Pete said, holding out his badge and ID.

"I heard about Barrett, and you can't pin that on me!"

With his back to Cameron and stepping toward Kimberly, Martin said, "How about giving me a tour of your house? It's beautiful."

Kimberly smiled, and they headed for the basement.

Attempting to get Cameron calmed down and reduce the tension, Pete said, "Great house. Are you the original owners?"

Relaxing his shoulders a hint, Cam said, "Yeah, because I'm an electrical contractor, I heard about the development while it was still on the drawing boards. Worked a deal with the developer, and my company is doing the electric for all the homes. We'll be doing the same for his next development. It's a real coup." He smiled. "You might as well sit down," he added. "Let's get this over with."

Cam returned to the couch, and Pete sat on an overstuffed chair facing him. Cam explained he got into electrical contracting by working for his dad, eventually buying into his dad's company, and over time buying out his dad.

Then Pete got down to the reason he and Martin were there, asking, "Why would I think you had anything to do with Dave's death? Why not help me clear your name?"

"Like you'll believe me."

"I hate it when people prejudge me," Pete said. "How about you?"

"For sure."

"I heard you and Barrett got into a scuffle yesterday."

"Yeah! Have you ever been audited by the IRS?"

"No, and I hope it never happens."

"Well, thanks to Dave, they're now after me. I freaked when I saw the letter." Cam sighed and ran his fingers through his hair.

"I would too," Pete sympathized and added, "I understand Dave got bailed out last night. How about you?"

"Yeah, my wife got me out."

"Your arraignment was today?"

"Yes, and I barely got there on time. Overslept, then had to contend with rush hour traffic. Everyone who lives in Wisconsin must work in either downtown Minneapolis or downtown St. Paul."

Pete nodded and said, "Can't tell you how happy I am that it doesn't affect my commute. And I understand why you might have overslept. Spending a few hours in jail can drain a guy."

"And Kimberly spent a lot of time last night salving my ego and helping me feel better." Remer grinned.

"Did you drive yourself to the courthouse?"

"Yeah.

"What time did you leave?"

"A little after 8:00."

"Did your wife go with you?"

Cameron shook his head. "She wanted to, but she had to be at work at 7:00."

"What time did she leave?" Pete asked.

"Around 6:50. She doesn't have much of a commute."

"Where does she work?"

"What does that have to do with anything?"

"I'm working on getting a complete picture. Why are you unwilling to say?"

"I'm not! She works at the doggy day care on the way from here to I-94. When people leave town, they often drop off their dogs early. That's why she starts so early."

Pete noticed the place on the way here and wondered how his dog Benji would react to being dropped off there. Kimberly might make it bearable, if her responsibilities included cuddling for hours with the puppies.

"What time did you leave?" Pete asked again.

"Around 8:00. I can't be more specific than that."

"See any neighbors on your way out the door or out of the development?"

"Naw. Never do."

"What time was your arraignment?"

"9:00."

"What time did you arrive at the courthouse?"

"8:57. Like I said, rush hour traffic is always a nightmare, and there was a major slowdown, due to an accident by Signal Hills. What time did Dave die?"

"It's an active investigation, so I can't say. When was the last time you saw Dave, before yesterday?"

"Monday afternoon. I went to his office and showed him the letter I received from the IRS."

"Did you have an appointment?"

"No."

"What time did you meet with him?"

"Around 3:00."

"Where did you go from there?"

Remer thought a minute, then said, "I just hung around downtown. Stopped at the Subway in the skyway and checked out a few shops."

"Did you notice anyone hanging around his office?"

"No, but I had just one thing on my mind, and I wasn't paying attention to anyone or anything else."

"How often did you see or speak with Dave?"

"Only when I had tax or bookkeeping questions or issues."

"And how often was that?"

"Several times each year."

"Can you think of anyone, a neighbor, friend, or family member, who might know what time you left this morning? For instance, perhaps a neighbor retrieved their newspaper, looked out their window, opened their garage door to leave, anything like that to provide you with an alibi?"

Cameron gave Pete a hands-up shrug. "If so, I'm not aware of it."

"Did Dave ever give you a ride downtown?"

"No."

"I'm trying to remember, where did he park while at his office?"

"Cute. I'll bet a hundred dollars you know as well as I do."

"How did you know what time he'd go to his car? Did you follow him?"

Remer stared at him angrily and said nothing.

"Did you get or make any calls between the time Kimberly left for work and you arrived at the courthouse this morning?"

"I called my attorney after I parked and was about to run to the courthouse. That had to be about 8:52. Want me to find it on my phone?"

"Please, and while doing that, it wouldn't hurt to check and make sure you aren't forgetting any calls."

Remer pulled a cellphone out of a hip pocket of his chinos, pressed several buttons, then looked up and said,

"8:50, and no other incoming or outgoing calls before 9:30 this morning."

"Where did you and Dave brawl yesterday?"

Cam bit his lip, sighed, and stared into space, considering. Finally, he said, "That has nothing to do with his death."

"Nonetheless, where did it happen?"

Attempting to stare Pete down, Cam asked, "Where was Dave attacked this morning?"

Pete knew that information had probably already been released but said, "Like I said, it's ..."

Cam rolled his eyes and said, "I know. It's an active investigation and *blah, blah, blah.*"

Pete nodded and asked again where he and Dave fought.

"You know, and I know, you could look it up in the reports."

"And you won't say because?"

Remer shook his head in disgust and said, "It was in the parking ramp where he parked his car when at work."

"The Robert Street ramp has six floors. How did you happen to cross paths?"

Cam stared at Pete and remained silent.

"Who threw the first punch?" Pete asked.

"That had nothing to do with his death. I had nothing to do with his death! I've had enough. What happened to your partner?" he asked, stood, and hollered, "Kimberly!"

Pete stood, hoping Kimberly had cooperated with Martin.

She appeared in the doorway to the office, smiled, and said, "I was just wondering if you're finished, Dear. I don't want the pork chops to be dried out and tough."

Pete smiled and said, "Thanks for your time, Mr. Remer. My partner and I will get out of your hair." They each gave him a business card, just in case ...

Kimberly escorted them out the front door and to the double garage, where she entered a code in the keypad and waited for it to open. Then she stepped inside, grabbed a paver from the stack around the corner and to the right, and handed it to Martin. Turning to Pete, she said, "I hope Cam wasn't too belligerent. I know he didn't do it. He isn't crazy enough to ruin his life and mine."

In the privacy of the unmarked car, Martin shared his findings with Pete.

"When she bailed him out, he was still furious with Barrett and insisted he'd finish the job. She explained that meant completing the battle, not killing him. He hadn't yet showered when she left for work just before 7:00. When I found out where she worked, I asked if she ever noticed passing cars while at work. She said rarely, and she didn't see her husband's car this morning. She doubts any of the neighbors saw him leave. She did say no matter how angry Cam was, he'd beat up someone, but he could never kill anyone. They liked the pavers Dave and Melissa had around their shrubs, found out where they purchased them, and bought the same ones from the same store—Menards. They don't have any gardening gloves. They hire someone to do all their yard work."

It was 6:10, so before Martin started the car, they discussed the next, best steps.

"Try Edgar Waltham, again?" Pete asked. "Based on what his sister said, he should be home by now. If he isn't, we'll try Gordon Shevlin. Martin, at times like this, I wish Teddy didn't now sleep through the night. I won't get home until after he's in bed. Previously, at least I'd see him when he woke us up every few hours for a feeding."

"The old forty-eight-hour rule, huh?" Martin said. "That's why we push so hard to get as far as we can as fast as we can." As he said that, he thought of a solution, albeit a poor one. "You could always put him back on a diet of nothing but milk."

"Great idea—not. Teddy loves some of the tastes, and he'd never forgive me. He might even ask Katie to give me a timeout until he's two and can tell me what he thinks of my antics."

"You don't think he'll be able to give you a piece of his mind before he turns two?" Martin chuckled.

"Can you imagine Katie's reaction if I came home with a suggestion like that?"

"Yes, I sure can. She'd laugh, knowing you're kidding."

With their plan of attack in place, Martin headed for their next destination. He didn't mention dinner. He decided to leave that up to Pete. Maybe they'd work a few more hours and head home ... he hoped.

Traveling west on I-94, without the companionship rush hour traffic would have offered had they been going the other way, Pete said, "Okay, Martin, here are my thoughts on Remer. Yesterday, he attacked Barrett in the Robert Street ramp, not the other way around. To do so, he either had to follow him or lie in wait. Of special consideration is the fact it looks like the person who murdered him lay in wait for him to open the garage door."

"Of course, that doesn't mean Remer murdered him. It means only that it matches the pattern he used previously. I wish we'd gotten a search warrant and had his home and car searched before we met with him. If he attacked Barrett this morning and hadn't already done so, I'll bet right now he's busy disposing of any clothing or gloves, as well as the screwdriver or whatever was used to pry loose the paver at Barrett's."

ELEVEN

Edgar Waltham

Wanting to make good use of the twenty-minute drive from Lake Elmo to Frogtown, Pete called the phone number Macalester College provided for Mike Hinckley. It was 7:10 in Maryland, and that seemed like an acceptable time to call a working man.

"The number you have reached is no longer in service," said a voice that approximated the human voice better than some people he knew. That meant he had to wait until he got the contact information from Barrett's cellphone, computer, or other electronic device, courtesy of Forensics.

He had some additional questions for Joel Milroy, but decided to wait until Martin could pay better attention and participate in the conversation. So he asked Martin, "How is Marty doing?"

"He loves high school. Signed up for driver's ed, and he's counting the days until he gets his license. Michelle and I are less enthused." Martin shook his head. "Think what it'll do to the cost of our insurance. Remember a year ago when he took his friends for a joy ride?"

"What I remember most is how happy you were, after you had a heart-to-heart with him and he promised it wouldn't happen again. I'm glad Teddy will never do anything like that."

Martin started singing "Beautiful Dreamer."

"Well, a guy can hope."

"And a guy should do his best to stay in touch with reality. Speaking of reality, last summer, Marty announced his plans to try out for the football team. Michelle and I spent an entire Sunday afternoon telling him we forbade it and why. We pulled up the statistics on chronic traumatic encephalopathy. We showed him the results of the brain scans from deceased pros who donated their brains to the research, before we got through to him. I'm glad he couldn't have played without our permission. Otherwise, anticipating our reaction, he'd probably have signed up and not bothered to tell us. We convinced him to try out for soccer instead. I'm happy to say, he made the cut. See what you have to look forward to, Pete?"

Pete smiled and said, "Teddy's six months old. Let's not rush things."

"By returning today," Martin said as he and Pete approached Elaine Waltham's apartment building, "we may be giving Waltham too much power."

"How so?"

"Currently, we are batting a thousand, when it comes to finding the people we want to speak with. Waltham has the power to drop that to 750. Seriously, Pete, should we grant anyone that much power?"

"Our other option?"

"Well," Martin shrugged, "we could always go home."

"Or stay the course and trust in the power of positive thinking."

Reaching Elaine's door, they heard voices coming from within. Feeling optimistic and hoping it didn't mean Elaine was on the phone or relying on the TV for companionship again, Martin knocked and held his breath.

Soon they heard the sounds of the chain and the deadbolt. Then the door opened and Elaine said, "Saw you through the peephole and recognized you. I told Edgar to expect you. I didn't think you'd be back today. I hope this isn't cause for concern."

"No," Pete said. "It only means we were nearby and, based on what you said this afternoon, hoped to find Edgar."

"Well, you succeeded, but I'm not sure he's ready to talk to you. He's had another rough day."

"Sorry to hear that," Martin said. "We'll make it as brief as possible."

"Okay, come on in," she said.

As she stepped to the side, a tired looking, fifty-year-old man approached. He was just shy of six feet with an average build, salt-and-pepper hair, brown eyes with drooping lids, a large nose, and a square jaw. He did not have a rose-colored birthmark on his right cheek. Not even one disguised with makeup. "Hear you're looking for me," he said. "Let's get it over with."

He led them into the living room.

Elaine followed.

Pete wondered if she thought Edgar might need her protection.

Elaine and Edgar sat on the couch. Pete and Martin took the overstuffed chairs.

"I'd offer you something to drink, but I'm confident you won't be here long enough for that," Elaine said.

Setting the ground rules? Pete wondered.

"I heard about David Barrett," Edgar said. "Guess the timing for my release from Stillwater couldn't have been worse, huh?"

"How so?" Martin asked.

"Please, don't treat me like an idiot. You're here because you think I killed him. Had I been released just two weeks later, you'd have had to look elsewhere."

"You aren't a suspect yet," Martin said, "but in light of the threats you made before you were convicted, we need to follow up."

Edgar sat slump shouldered and said, "I was falsely accused and convicted, but I know you aren't here about that. All I can tell you is I lost ten years of my life, and I'm *not* going back to prison. Barrett saw a guy dressed the way I was and assumed I was the person he saw attacking that woman. He was wrong. He never got a good look at her attacker's face. He couldn't have, because it wasn't me, and I never saw him before the trial. I don't know what happened to the man he saw, but the way I was dressed wasn't unique. And I wasn't even in the Golden Rule Building that day. Sorry, I'll shut up. This isn't helping you or me. What do you want to know?"

"Sounds like a good reason to hate the man responsible for your conviction," Pete said.

"Do you have any idea what it would do to you if you let something like that eat away at you for a decade? It would make that decade seem like an eternity. I moved on. My survival depended upon it."

"Are you married?" Martin asked.

"Was. Divorced her several months before my conviction."

"Have you seen or communicated with her since your conviction?" Martin asked.

"I heard from her, occasionally, about the kids, for the first two years. Saw her after that when she brought our son Zach every few months for a visit. She made it clear they were there only because otherwise he was impossible. She never brought our daughter, and I doubt Wendy remembers me. She was only two when I was locked away."

"How old was Zach?" Martin asked.

"Seven."

"Have you seen Wendy since you were released?" Martin asked.

Edgar bit his lip, shook his head, and said, "My ex knows I'm out, and hasn't said or done anything to help me reconnect with Wendy. She's only twelve, so it can't happen without my ex's help or approval. Maybe she knows what's best for our daughter, but I'd sure like to see her. I'm so thankful for Zach. Can't even imagine life without him—and Elaine." Edgar smiled at her.

Martin noticed tears in Elaine's eyes.

"Unfortunately," Edgar continued, "Zach inherited my tendency towards impatience. He can't understand why I'm having so much trouble finding a job. And he's angry that, due to the requirements for a background check and my felony conviction, I can never again be a paramedic or an EMT. It hurts. I loved that work." Edgar sighed and shook his head. "Right now, almost anything would sound good. However, I'm not yet desperate enough to become a dishwasher or a waste disposal engineer. Check back next week."

"Have you seen or spoken with your ex-wife since you got out?" Martin asked.

Edgar grimaced and shook his head.

"How about Zach?" Martin asked.

Edgar smiled and nodded.

"When?" Martin asked.

"He called Elaine and found out I'm staying here. He's been here three times. We're expecting him tomorrow evening."

Both he and Elaine smiled.

Pete and Martin learned Zach was a sophomore at the U of M and in pre-med, even though he was only seventeen.

"He plans to be a general practitioner and set up a practice in a greater Minnesota community needing a doctor." Edgar beamed proudly.

Pete and Martin smiled and nodded.

"How do you get around these days?" Pete asked.

"MTC buses and the light rail."

"Have you been in the Golden Rule Building since your release?" Pete asked.

"Yes, a couple of times."

"Why did you go there?" Pete asked.

"You mean why did I return to the scene of the crime I didn't commit?" Edgar said resignedly.

"I wouldn't put it that way," Pete said. "But yes, why go there?"

Edgar straightened his shoulders, looked Pete in the eye, and said, "I was looking for David Barrett. I wanted to tell him I no longer hate him. It was important to me that he know that. Now he either knows or never will." Edgar shook his head.

Pete nodded and asked, "What time did you leave this morning?"

"How about answering that one for me, Elaine? They're more likely to believe you than me."

"I already told them, but if they want to check to see if I can remember what I said, in keeping with what has become his weekday schedule, he walked out the door at

7:50 to catch the Route 67 bus going east on Minnehaha to downtown."

"Do you ever loan him your car?" Martin asked.

This time, Edgar answered for her. "My driver's license expired while I was in prison. It takes forever, plus a week or two to get an appointment for a behind-the-wheel test. She refuses to let me borrow her car before I get it. Rather inflexible, wouldn't you say?" He smiled at her.

"Do you ever drive him?" Martin asked.

"Occasionally, but I haven't driven him anywhere since last week. In other words, since several days before the attack on David Barrett."

"Does Zach have a car?" Pete asked.

"You can't possibly think he ..." Edgar shouted angrily.

"He sounds like a great kid, and why would he?" Pete said. "It's a standard question. Please answer."

After a pause, getting his anger under control, Edgar spoke slowly and deliberately, "He has a 2000 Honda Civic with more than 200,000 miles on it. So he drives it only to school and to see Elaine and me."

"Color?" Pete asked.

Both investigators saw the steam rising from the top of Edgar's head as he said, "Red. And I hope you don't plan on hassling him!"

Pete hated to ask but did, "Where does he live?"

"With his mom ... my ex."

"Her name is?" Pete asked.

"Sandra Norcross. She got married two months after our divorce was finalized."

"Was that before or after you were convicted?" Pete asked, even though Elaine already told them.

"Before."

"And where does she live?" Pete asked.

"On St. Paul's East Side."

Pete and Martin made a note of the exact address, planning to interview her as well as Zachary.

After obtaining Zachary's and Sandra's phone numbers, Pete and Martin thanked Edgar and his sister.

With the door closing behind him, Pete turned back and asked Edgar, "You were a paramedic when you were convicted?"

Edgar nodded.

"Where?" Pete asked.

"St. Paul Fire Department."

"Who was your supervisor?"

"Charlie Odin, and what difference does that make? There's nothing he can do to help."

TWELVE
Gordon Shevlin, Jealous Husband

The two investigators hoofed it to Martin's unmarked car, shaking their heads. "It's 6:45," Pete said. "Should we check to see if we can go five for five?"

"Why not? We have four locations on our list. Should we start with the closest and work our way south, or at the southernmost location and work our way north?"

"I hate to sound like a pessimist, but how about starting with the closest one, Gordon Shevlin? Then we can work our way south through Barrett's in-laws. Once we either fail to find or finish with his wife's sister in Lakeville, we can work our way back, making a second attempt at the place or places where we failed on our way south."

"I see one problem with that plan, Pete."

"And that is?"

"It assumes we won't succeed on our first visit to each location. It's Tuesday evening. Other than sitting and waiting for us, what could these people be doing?"

Pete shook his head and slid into the unmarked car.

Martin started the car, took Lexington Avenue to I-94. Then he went east to the Highway 52 exits, and went south to Wentworth Avenue.

On the way, they discussed their last stop. Pete started by saying, "You know what, Martin? In light of what Beth told us, I think he's telling the truth. I don't think he attacked that woman in the Golden Rule Building."

"Pete, he had ten years to rehearse that speech."

"He did, but I don't believe he's that good an actor or a sociopath. I also believe he and his sister told the truth about this morning. How about you?"

"But wouldn't you be bitter if someone's mistake cost ten years of your life and quite possibly your chances for happiness going forward?"

"Absolutely, and I'd wonder why a little divine intervention didn't save me. But like he said, it's wasted time and energy. Not only does it fail to change what happened, it also takes a toll on every day going forward. I think he came to that realization. Based on his body language and the way he looked at us, I don't think he read it in a book or heard it somewhere and memorized it."

"I suspect you're right and, like he said, he didn't have to be the only one dressed that way the day the woman was attacked. Also, whereas it should narrow the field, he didn't have to be the only one dressed that way and carrying a gun." Martin shook his head. "But what about the purse?" he asked.

"Let's say you stole a purse. How far would you carry it before you tossed it in a trash can, a mailbox, or anywhere convenient?"

"No further than I absolutely had to. But what about fingerprints? Wouldn't the attacker have left them on the purse? Wouldn't fingerprints have cleared Waltham?"

"Unless the guy pulled his sweatshirt down over his hand or wore gloves," Pete said.

"Or," Martin said, "dropped it somewhere, and someone picked it up and walked away with it. Or for some unknown reason, they just never found it."

Martin followed Wentworth to Gordon Shevlin's neighborhood of homes built in the 1950s and 1960s on half-acre lots—give or take a few square feet. His was a two-story with honey-beige brick on the lower level, white vinyl siding on the second floor, and an attached double garage on the right side. The trim and garage door were white. The front door was red. White lights stood to the right and left of the front door and the garage door.

A large fern occupied a spot on the left side of the lot near the street. A variety of shrubs grew unchecked beneath the double-hung windows on the left. The number of bicycles discarded on the lawn competed with the number of skateboards.

Taking a deep breath, Martin rang the doorbell, hoping neither the failure to get a response nor a swarm of kids would derail their plans.

As he prepared to press the button a second time, a red-haired woman who appeared to be in her late thirties opened the door. She was trim and about five feet five with hazel eyes, a button nose, and full red lips.

The two investigators identified themselves and displayed their badges and IDs.

When Martin asked, "Ms. Shevlin?" she nodded and said, "Yes, Angela."

"Can we come in?" he asked. "We have some questions for you and Gordon."

After hesitating, she said, "Sure," and stepped aside, making room for them.

They entered a foyer with a brown tile floor and beige walls. On the left stood a ten-foot-long wall, followed by a stairway to the second floor.

Angela led them past the stairway to a large family room on the right with knotty pine hardwood floors. As they entered, a picture window with faded gold curtains filled the wall to their right. Straight ahead stood a white, brick fireplace with a raised hearth.

Boxy, dark and medium-brown striped velour chairs with rounded arms faced the fireplace, and a curved, bright-yellow couch that took up half the room faced the windows. LEGOs and matchbox cars covered most of the floor space.

"Please forgive the mess," Angela said, blushing. "We weren't expecting company. Have a seat, and I'll get Gordy."

The house seemed quieter than anticipated, and Pete and Martin wondered if homework had the full attention of their kids.

They stood, backs to the sofa, so they'd see anyone entering the room. Several seconds later, they heard a light tread descend the stairs, followed by a significantly heavier one. Angela appeared in the doorway, looking rattled.

Gordon stood behind her, looking perturbed. Per his driver's license, he was forty years old, five feet eight and one hundred eighty-five pounds. He had brown eyes framed by glasses with thick, black frames, and wore a thin-lipped expression. His chinos and blue-striped shirt were wrinkled, and sweat decorated the underarms of his shirt.

"Aren't you supposed to make appointments?" he growled.

"You're Gordon?" Pete asked.

Gordon nodded impatiently.

"We were in the neighborhood and have a few questions for you and your wife," Pete said. Then he and Martin introduced themselves.

"And maybe this isn't a good time." Gordon glared.

"No problem, Mr. Shevlin," Pete said. "We'll stop in to see you tomorrow at work."

Gordon shrunk a bit and said, "Well, as long as you're here, we might as well get it over with. What do you want to know?"

"While you and I talk," Pete said, "my partner will speak with your wife. That will shorten the amount of time required.

Gordon opened his mouth, then closed it and nodded. "Take him downstairs to the family room, Angie," he instructed.

"I worry about the cars and other junk that could be on the stairs," she said, looking at the floor. "What if he steps on something and loses his footing?"

"Then take him into the dining room," he said, shaking his head.

Martin followed Angie out of the room.

Gordon sat on the sofa, so Pete sat on one of the chairs.

After crossing his arms across his chest, Gordon said, "Okay, let's get this over with."

"I understand you and David Barrett were friends," Pete said.

Gordon jumped up. Weight on his toes and fists clenched, face transitioning to scarlet, he snarled, "Is that what this is about? I know Dave was murdered this morning. Do you think that has something to do with me? It doesn't! I didn't appreciate the way he started hustling Angie after Melissa died, but surely you don't think I'd solve it that way!"

Thanks to that outburst, Pete got a good whiff of Gordon's breath and thought, *It smells like he has a blood alcohol level at least twice the legal limit.* "In that case," he said, "help me clear your name. Where were you this morning between 6:00 and 8:30?"

"I was here until 7:20, then I left for work."

"Where do you work?"

"For the City of St. Paul, in Public Works."

"Did you drive?"

"Of course."

"Did anyone ride with you?"

"No." Gordon sighed, knowing what that meant.

"Do you have an alibi?"

"Angie and four of our kids know I was here until 7:20."

"How many kids do you have?"

"Six."

"Ages?" Pete asked.

"Angie's better at this than me. It's harder than you might think. It changes so fast." He counted them off slowly on his fingers: "Gordy is fifteen, Ginger is thirteen, Jessica is twelve, Jayden is ten, Chloe is eight, and Noah is seven."

"Which ones saw you leave this morning?"

"The four youngest: Jessie, Jayden, Chloe, and Noah."

"You work in downtown St. Paul?" Pete asked.

Gordon nodded.

"What time did you arrive at work?"

"7:55."

"Did anyone see you arrive?"

"Yeah, a couple of my buddies."

"Did anyone see you between here and downtown? Maybe someone you passed along the way or who passed and looked over at you?"

"No one I know. I see a lot of the same cars every day, but I don't know who drives any of them or if they'd remember me."

"It takes thirty-five minutes to get downtown from here?"

"It takes between fifteen and thirty minutes. Have you ever seen the traffic headed north on Highway 52 during the morning rush hour? Approaching the Lafayette Bridge, it's a nightmare. Dumbest design ever. For that reason, I take city streets all the way. Since I never know exactly how long it will take, I have to allow for worst case, and I need to allow another five minutes to park and walk to the office."

"Which streets?" Pete asked.

"Robert Street all the way," Gordon said as he stood, walked over to the floor lamp, and turned it on high. The sun was setting and natural light no longer sufficed.

"What did you do between 7:55 and 8:30?"

"Stared at my computer monitor."

"Can anyone back up that claim?"

"The person at the front desk. I'd have had to pass him to get out the door."

"There isn't another entrance or exit?" Pete knew that would be a violation of the fire code.

"There's an emergency exit, but using it would have raised a commotion and announce my departure to everyone in the office at the time."

Pete noted the name of the person who sat at the front desk this morning, between 7:55 and 8:30, as well as the phone number to reach the front desk.

"What do you drive these days?"

"A Kia Optima."

"Year and color?"

"2017 and red. They call it Remington Red."

"And your wife?" Pete asked.

"She has a dark-blue Chevy Fusion."

Pete thanked Gordon and asked if it was okay if he stayed put until Martin returned.

Gordon gave him a hands-up shrug and left him sitting there.

Before Pete finished his notes for that meeting, Martin joined him, smiling.

THIRTEEN

Angela Shevlin, Jealous Husband's Wife

M artin waited until they were back in his unmarked car to share the results of his interview.

"Angela began by apologizing profusely for the condition of their home," he said. "She wasn't referring just to the toys lying around. They have six kids. Money is tight even though they both have good jobs. Plus they're dealing with the looming threat of putting six kids through college. By the way, she goes from home to home, providing physical therapy to the homebound."

"Then," Martin continued, "she told me all about last Sunday and the incident Clark described, when Gordon threatened Barrett. She referred to it as a threat. She said Gordon drank too much, and more often than she cares to remember, that's a problem. When he does, he gets antagonistic, argumentative, and belligerent. But she insisted it never results in more than a verbal attack."

"She claimed full responsibility for what happened at the restaurant. Sounds a lot like the victims of spousal abuse, doesn't it? I asked if he ever laid a hand on her, and she said 'NEVER!' She said she's always liked Dave Barrett, but only as a friend. She's worried about him ever since he cut himself off from all his married friends after Melissa died. For that reason, she spent a lot of that night looking at him, hoping to make eye contact—so she could invite him over to their table. She dared not walk over and talk to him. That would have made Gordon even more explosive."

"According to Angela, when they got home Sunday night, she spent a lot of time assuring Gordon he's the only one for her. She explained she was looking at Dave only because of her concern for him. She just wanted to know that he's doing okay. According to her, Gordon accepted that and felt foolish about his outburst."

"Taking notes?" Martin smiled. "Almost finished. She said Gordon left at 7:20 this morning, give or take a minute or two. He always leaves at that time. She and four of her kids saw him walk out the door."

"Finally, she knew about Barrett. Someone in Gordon's office has public radio running whenever he's at work. He knew Gordon and Dave were friends and told Gordon about it as soon as he heard. Gordon called her immediately. He was upset about the way he treated Dave on Sunday, and the fact he could never apologize. She said he broke down and begged for her assurances he wasn't a complete jackass."

While Martin drove to Inver Grove Heights, Pete checked a trip planner on his cellphone. It indicated the trip from the Shevlin home to David Barret's, during the morning rush hour, would take about twenty-five minutes. So Gordon might have had just enough time to get to Barrett's home and murder him as he headed out the door. However, there was no way he could do that and reach the office by 7:55.

Tomorrow he and Martin would check with the person at the front desk about Shevlin's arrival time this morning.

FOURTEEN

Tim and Dorothy Peterson, Dave's Father- & Mother-in-Law

"Time for the in-laws," Martin said. "I hope our luck holds."

"Luck?" Pete asked. "Did I just hear you referring to today's successes as luck? It's known as planning, Martin."

"Oh, like planning for these people to be home?"

"Exactly. Have we ever approached a location planning for the person we want to interview to not be there?"

Martin shook his head, laughing. He'd never win this one.

The trip from South St. Paul to Inver Grove Heights barely gave Martin and Pete time to discuss the next planned interviews. Again they'd split up husband and wife, guarding against the answers of one influencing the responses of the other.

Martin took Seventh Avenue to Inver Grove Heights, where the street name changed to Cahill. He stayed on Cahill for about a half mile, then went left on Burnham Circle and into the Timber Hills Retirement Community. Identical townhomes with two-car garages stood in front of and on both sides of him and Pete. After he parked in a guest parking slot, they walked to the Petersons' large, two-level townhome.

Since the sun had set, interior lights provided an indication, though possibly a false one, that Tim and/or Dorothy was home. The abundance of people relying on automatic timers made it far less reliable than it once was.

"Let's find out how Dave Barrett's in-laws felt about him," Martin said, reaching for the doorbell.

A woman who appeared to be in her seventies looked out the flanking window, then opened the door and asked, "Can I help you?"

Pete and Martin identified themselves and showed her their badges and IDs.

She nodded and said, "I'm Dorothy Peterson. Are you here about David? We saw the reports on the news and instantly recognized his and Melissa's home. We've been waiting for someone from the police department to come and tell us what happened. Ever since his dad died and his mom took off, we've been like substitute parents for Dave. We love him like a son." She brushed away a tear. "Tim will be sorry he missed you."

Dorothy was five foot three and roly-poly. She had snow-white hair, pale skin, bright-red glasses that drew attention to her bright-blue eyes, and a round face. She wore navy sweat pants and a baggy pale-blue top.

"We're so sorry for your loss," Pete said. "Did you hear from either of David's brothers today?"

"No, but we weren't close to them, and they must have their hands full."

"We're trying to determine what happened to David and have some questions for you and your husband," Pete said.

"Oh," she said, sounding surprised. Then she quickly added, "Come in. Tim will be home any minute. He's walking a neighbor home. He's too much of a gentleman to let her walk home alone after dark, even though, with all the automatic lights, it never really gets dark here. I love June, when the sun sets two hours later than now."

She smiled, opened the screen door, and waved them in.

They followed her through the foyer with tan ceramic tile flooring and into the great room with medium-beige carpeting. The kitchen was on the left. A large dining room table, eight chairs, and a hutch filled the space between the kitchen and the living room area. Beyond it was a deck looking out on lots of trees surrounding a pond.

Dorothy ushered Pete and Martin over to a couple of overstuffed flowered chairs. She sat across from them on an avocado-colored Mediterranean-style sofa. Across the room stood two plaid recliners, with a large table stocked with books between them. It appeared that pairing down their furniture when they moved here might have been a challenge.

As Pete and Martin waited for her to get settled, Dorothy said, "Dave was a wonderful husband and son-in-law. Melissa often told Tim and me how lucky she was to be his wife. They celebrated their tenth anniversary a month before she died. Dave didn't leave her side the last month," Dorothy said, as tears streamed down her cheeks. "He still hadn't recovered. We were very close to her, and Dave has spent a lot of time with Tim and me ever since she passed. I think he felt that being with us was as close as he could get to being with Melissa. Sorry, I'll stop rambling. Losing Dave is a shock, and it feels like we just lost another child." Dorothy pulled a tissue from a pocket and dabbed at her eyes.

"When did you last see Dave?" Pete asked.

"He went to Mass with us last Sunday and we went out for brunch. Tim's and my fiftieth anniversary will be next June, and Dave asked where we'd like to go after the party, sort of a second honeymoon. That gives you an idea of the kind of person he is. If our own son and daughter are thinking about it, neither has said a word to Tim or me." She sighed.

"Was Dave close to your son and other daughter?" Martin asked.

"I don't think Matt or Amy spent much time with him. Between their jobs and Matt's children, I don't know where they'd have found the time. I know they'll regret that now." She sniffed.

"Also," she added, staring at her lap, "both were close to Melissa. That may have made it difficult to be around Dave. Too many memories, you know. I think Amy had a crush on Dave when he and Melissa first began dating. I think she even fantasized about marrying him. And Matt used to blame Dave for Melissa's death. There is no history of cancer in my family or Tim's. Matt said Melissa's cancer was caused by the stress she and Dave were under in the days preceding the trial where Dave testified as the eyewitness. The whole family was on edge those days, not knowing if the animal who did it would hurt or kill Dave and/or Melissa."

"Do you think Matt might have been right?" Pete asked.

"Well, I think stress can weaken a person's immune system, but I don't think it's anything as simple as stress leads to or results in cancer."

"You said you spent a lot of time with Dave," Pete said. "Did he talk about his business?"

"Not really. He just said he liked his downtown location because lots of the people working downtown came to see him on their lunch breaks."

"A lot of people might take advantage of that by opening up late in the morning," Pete said. "Did Dave?"

"I remember telling him I'd like a job I didn't have to start before noon. He said he still opened the office at 8:00, because some people who didn't start until 9:00 preferred to come in earlier."

"It doesn't sound like you're an early riser." Martin smiled.

"I'm not, Tim is. He's always up at 6:30. He showers, shaves, reads the newspaper, and has coffee brewing by the time I get out of bed. I think it became ingrained while he was working. Anyway, it hasn't changed. I got up early every morning when our kids were young and when Tim still left for work at about 7:30. Now I'm doing what comes natural for me. I get up about 9:00. If that bothered Tim, I'd get up earlier. I'm glad it doesn't."

"Were you on your normal schedule this morning?" Martin asked.

"Yup."

"Can you think of anyone who might want to hurt Dave?" Pete asked.

Dorothy propped her chin on her right fist and stared at the floor. After several seconds, she looked up and said, "I can't think of anyone. But, other than his and Melissa's wedding and her funeral, I never saw him with his friends. And I don't know any of them. I suppose it could have something to do with his accounting business, but I know nothing about that or his clients. Sorry I can't be more helpful."

Seeing Pete tuck his notepad in a pocket inside his suitcoat, Dorothy said, "I assume you want to wait for Tim. He should be here any second. I'm surprised it's taken so long. Judy must have needed his help with something. If you don't have any additional questions for me, while we wait, can I get you something to drink?"

"That would be appreciated," Martin said. He was surprised Pete and Dorothy couldn't hear his stomach growling. Or maybe Dorothy did, and that was why she made the offer.

She stood and said, "Let's go into the dining room. Then you'll have a convenient place to set your beverages. What sounds good to you? We have pretty much everything, from lime sparkling water, to regular and Diet Coke, to hot or iced tea, to hot or iced coffee."

"How about a Diet Coke?" Pete and Martin said simultaneously, and Dorothy laughed.

"Can I help you carry them into the dining room?" Pete asked.

"That depends. They're refrigerated. Even so, would you like a glass of ice?"

Pete and Martin said they'd drink it out of the cans, so Dorothy told them to have a seat, and she'd be right back.

"You have a lovely home," Pete said when she returned and handed each an ice-cold can. "How long have you lived here?"

Before Dorothy could answer, the three of them heard the front door close.

Dorothy called out, "Tim, we have company. Please join us."

Tim Peterson was tall and slender with a headful of pepper-and-salt hair. He had large brown eyes, a Roman nose, and an inquisitive smile. He too appeared to be in his seventies, stood ramrod straight, and moved swiftly and confidently. He wore dress slacks and a striped shirt. He was stocking-footed, and Pete wondered if he should have removed his shoes. Dorothy wore slippers, but ...

Tim walked over to Dorothy, put an arm around her and asked, "To what do we owe the pleasure?"

"They're police officers, Dear," Dorothy said, grasping the hand that rested on her shoulder. "They're here about Dave."

Tim's smile evaporated and he bent down, kissed her cheek, and said, "Sorry I wasn't here when they arrived, Dotty."

"No need to be. They've been very kind."

Pete and Martin introduced themselves. Then turning to Dorothy, Martin said, "I'm anxious to hear about this complex, how well you like it, the type of activities available, whether your grandkids are permitted to spend the night. All kinds of things like that. My parents are looking at places like this. Can we stay here and talk, while my partner speaks with your husband?"

She hesitated, then said, "Why not?"

After taking a long drink from his Diet Coke, Pete held it up and said, "I'll leave this here."

"No, take it with you." Dorothy smiled. She reached behind her, grabbed a coaster, and handed it to him.

Pete thanked her and followed Tim down the stairs to the family room. Tim sat on a striped loveseat, and Pete sat across from him on a highbacked leather chair.

Relying on a system that had served him well in situations like this, Pete opened with a question meant to put Tim at ease. "What do you or did you do for a living?" he asked.

Tim smiled and said. "I'm a physician ... an endocrinologist, if you want me to be more specific."

"Interesting. Were you with a group or did you have your own practice?"

"I was with Park Nicollet. After I retired, Dotty and I moved here. We wanted to be closer to the kids."

"How long ago did you retire?"

"Seven years ago. In June of 2012. The kids bought us a trip for a retirement gift. We spent two weeks in England and France. It was wonderful."

When asked the last time he saw Dave, Tim provided the same answer as his wife.

"How did he seem that day?" Pete asked. "Was he more anxious or nervous than usual?"

Tim shook his head and said, "In fact, he was bubbling over, planning for our fiftieth anniversary. It was the most relaxed I'd seen him since his wife, our daughter Melissa, died. He took her death very hard, and I got the impression he'd finally turned the corner and was beginning to bounce back. Losing her was hard on all of us, but especially Dave, of course. She was his world. Anyone who saw them together would know that. And after ten years, the way they looked at each other, you'd have thought they were still newlyweds. Unfortunately, with a lot of help from my son Matt, Dave blamed himself for her death."

"Why would he do that?"

"I'm sure you've heard all about Dave being threatened if he testified at a trial, but did so anyway. It was the right thing to do. We can't allow criminals to scare us out of prosecuting them. Can you imagine what kind of world that would be?"

Tim reiterated Dorothy's story about Matt blaming Dave for Melissa's death and said, "I told them there's no proof the stress she was under had anything to do with her cancer. Matt ignored me. He and Melissa were very close, and he had a hard time accepting her death. I think he was looking for a scapegoat." Tim sighed and shook his head.

"Dave had trouble believing me," he continued. "He suspected I'd have said that whether or not it was true, in an effort to help him. That, of course, is true. Dotty and I love that boy. The good news is, he and Melissa are reunited. I'm sure she greeted him with open arms." Tim bit his lower lip and nodded, choking back tears.

"I'm so grateful they didn't leave any orphans. They were working on starting a family when Melissa's cancer was discovered. The chemo forced them to place those plans on hold, then abandon them." Tim sighed.

Like Dorothy, Tim knew of no one who might be angry with or attack Dave. And like her, he knew none of Dave's friends, business associates, or clients.

"This is a standard question," Pete said, then asked, "Where were you and Dorothy between 6:30 and 9:00 this morning?"

Tim stared at him and said, "You mean you have to ask all the suspects, don't you?"

"It may seem that way but, depending on where you were, you could help by providing an alibi for someone else. That's why I'm asking."

"I got out of bed at 6:30. I always get out of bed at 6:30." Tim frowned. "Other than the minute or two I spent walking out on the driveway to get the morning paper, I was in the house and alone until Dorothy got up. No doubt she already told you that was at 9:00. No one calls before 9:00, out of courtesy to her. I didn't see her between about 7:00, when I left the bedroom and spent my time in the kitchen and living room. In other words," Tim said, crossing his arms over his chest, "she can't attest to my alibi, nor I to hers."

FIFTEEN
Matt Peterson,
Dave's Brother-in-Law

Based on the look on Pete's face, Martin figured Pete may have gotten the answers he needed in the meeting with Dr. Tim Peterson, but it didn't go well. He didn't ask about it. Pete would get around to it in good time.

"Okay, what do you think?" he asked, as first the Presbyterian Homes then Inver Grove Heights faded away in the rearview mirror.

"I think Dr. Peterson had plenty of time to get to Barrett's home, hit him over the head a few times with a brick, and get back to Inver Grove before Dorothy got up. I also think, being a retired doctor, he knew exactly where to hit him to kill him. He's strong enough to swing a paver with enough force to do it. He's capable of moving quietly enough to creep up on Barrett without being detected."

"You think he did it?" Martin asked.

"Could do it, yes. Did it, no."

"When it comes to in-laws," Martin said, "are the Petersons, or at least the version we saw, the norm or an anomaly? I have mixed emotions about mine, Pete. How do you feel about yours?"

"I didn't realize you're having problems with yours. What's the deal?"

"When Marty goes to them, looking for support for his stance on whatever, they almost always side with him. He knows better than to go to Michelle for a reversal of my decisions. The first words out of her mouth are always, 'What did your dad say?' Her parents rarely, if ever, consider that. I can guarantee they'd have been furious if their parents did that when Michelle was a teenager."

"Thankfully, I'm getting along well with mine," Pete said, "and I hope their dealings with Teddy never change that."

"What's your take on retirement communities?" Martin asked. "Do you plan on moving into one twenty or so years down the road?"

"Right now, I doubt it. I've always thought kids add something to a neighborhood. A little activity. A little ..."

"Noise and commotion?" Martin interrupted.

Pete laughed and said, "That too. Plus, if they don't allow kids, what will we do with Teddy's siblings, send them to live with you and Michelle?"

Martin rolled his eyes and said, "Thanks, but we'll be way too old to deal with kids by then."

The trip from Inver Grove to Burnsville provided enough time for Pete to reach out to Joel Milroy. He'd been Dave Barrett's attorney, during Edgar Waltham's trial. Pete didn't want to put it off any longer. So he dug out his cellphone.

Joel didn't answer and, because of their schedule, Pete didn't leave a message.

Meanwhile, Martin merged onto westbound I-494, exited onto southbound I-35E, and went right after exiting on County Road 11 in Burnsville. Then he went left on East 134ᵗʰ Street, right onto Walnut Drive, and wound his way around to Tim and Linda Petersons' neighborhood.

They lived in a dark-gray split level with white shutters, a large picture window on the right and a two-car garage on the left. The three-paneled front door had a window in the top panel.

As is often the case, trees in the front yards in this neighborhood looked to be the same age as the homes, which were built in the 1960s and 1970s. Junipers grew in front of the basement windows, and a maple on the front right corner of the lot must have spent the last forty years making up for lost time.

Their home was lit up like a Christmas tree, increasing Pete and Martin's optimism about another success today.

Sticking with their pattern or, in cop talk, their modus operandi or MO, Martin parked in front of the home two doors down from the Petersons. Then he and Pete continued their survey of the neighborhood on the way back to their destination.

In keeping with another pattern, Martin rang the doorbell as he and Pete positioned themselves to the right and left of the front door.

This time, a man came to the door. Based on his look of disgust, Pete wondered if his mom and dad gave him a heads up, regarding their interviews ... or interrogations, if that was how the family interpreted them.

"Matt Peterson?" Pete asked.

"Yeah. St. Paul cops?"

Pete and Martin answered by pulling and displaying their badges and IDs.

"Isn't it about time for you to call it a day?" Matt asked. He was forty-five, tall and slender, like his dad, had thick dark-brown hair and a five o'clock shadow, green eyes, and his father's Roman nose. He wore blue jeans and a black polo.

"We often have to work around the schedules of the people with whom we want to speak," Pete said.

"Terrific," Matt said, reached into a front pocket and pulled out an iPhone. "Since you're so accommodating, let me check to see what will work best for me."

"Unless your house is on fire or your wife or one of your kids is having a medical emergency, you'll make things work right now." Pete smiled.

"Now that you mention it, this will be perfect," Matt said and pushed open the door. Grinning, he added, "Mom said you were pretty smooth."

And what did your dad say? Pete wondered.

Matt took them up the four steps on the left side of the landing, and Pete and Martin saw the kitchen table, ceiling fan, and windows on the back of the house through French doors.

Then he led them to the right, along a railing, and into the family room with polished, honey-oak hardwood floors. Picture windows that looked out the front of the house filled the wall to their right. Straight ahead was an entertainment center with a large-screen TV.

An eight-foot-long, light-gray sofa stood in front of the windows. Two light-gray oversized chairs faced the entertainment center. Lamps on the end tables on either side of the sofa provided the only light in this room.

Once Pete and Martin were seated, Matt said, "Linda isn't here. She took the girls to a movie. All three were anxious to see *Downton Abbey*. Personally, I don't understand the popularity of the TV series, so I have no interest in the movie."

"How old are your daughters?" Martin asked.

"Eileen is fifteen. Clare is thirteen."

"Are they like my daughter, wanting at least two of every new style that comes out?" Martin fibbed. His daughter, Olivia, was still too young for that.

"Yes, but there's often little to no connection between what they want and what they get." He smiled.

"What do you do for a living?" Martin asked.

"I'm an environmental engineer at Flint Hills Resources in Rosemount."

"Do you have to commute to Rosemount every day?" Pete asked.

"Most days."

"That commute has to be a headache," Pete said.

"That's why I leave by 7:00 at the latest. Barely have a chance to say 'Hi' to Linda and the girls in the morning."

"Do you usually see them before you leave?" Pete asked, even though an alibi for 6:30 until 7:00 wouldn't go far.

"Sometimes yes, sometimes no. The girls are often just getting up, so I knock on their doors and tell them to have a good day. As for Linda, it all depends on her schedule. She's a dental hygienist and only has to be there when she has appointments. I should be so lucky." Matt glanced skyward.

"What time did you leave this morning?" Martin asked.

"At my usual time, 7:00. May have left a bit earlier. I was concerned about my commute. I had to go to White Bear Lake for a meeting with a contractor we were considering."

"What were you driving?" Pete asked.

"My company car, of course. It's a Ford Explorer."

"Color?" Martin asked.

"Charcoal."

"What does your wife drive?" Pete asked.

"A beige, 2018 Hyundai Accent."

"What's the contractor's name and phone number?" Martin asked.

"Before I say, you should know he may lie about the meeting, because I turned down his proposal."

"For that reason, he might deny your meeting?" Martin asked.

"He was angry that I rejected his proposal, so he might if he thought it could hurt me."

"How would that hurt you?" Martin asked.

"You're looking for an alibi, aren't you?"

"The name and phone number?" Martin repeated.

"Jerry Donnelly," Matt said and rattled off a phone number so fast that Martin had to ask him to repeat it.

"What's the name of his company, and where are they located?" Martin asked.

"Jerry Donnelly Consulting, White Bear Lake."

"Did you see your wife and daughters on your way out?" Martin asked.

"No, and no."

"Did you stop anywhere on your way to that meeting?" Martin asked.

Matt shook his head.

"Where and at what time were you scheduled to meet?" Martin asked.

"At 8:30 at Cafe Cravings. I warned him I might be a bit late, because I was unfamiliar with the rush-hour traffic between here and there. I was happy when I pulled into the parking lot a couple of minutes after 8:00. The traffic wasn't as bad as I'd imagined, there were no big pileups, and my GPS provided the fastest, but not very direct, route. It wasn't as bad as I'd anticipated, so I had to wait almost twenty minutes for him to show."

"When did you hear about Dave?" Pete asked.

"At lunch. A friend I work with knows he's my brother-in-law and heard about him. I didn't want Dad and Mom to hear about it over the phone, so I called Linda."

"How did Linda and Dave get along?" Pete asked.

"They rarely saw each other, but they liked each other. At least I know she liked him. I never heard her say anything bad about him. When I did, she sat quietly, not saying a word."

"And your daughters?" Pete asked.

"They love their Uncle Dave. He always asked how they were doing in school, about the books they were reading, and teased them about boys. Both broke down when they heard about him. I think Linda took them to a movie tonight to help take their minds off it."

"How about you, Matt?" Pete asked. "How did you feel about Dave?"

"Why ask me? I'm sure you already got the story from Dad and Mom."

"We prefer you answer the question," Martin said.

Matt rolled his eyes and said, "As you've already heard at least twice, I blame him for Melissa's death. Had he not been so gallant or self-righteous or whatever, he could have spared her the nights she was afraid to go to sleep, wondering if someone would break into their house and murder both of them. That lasted for months, between the arraignment and the trial. She became a walking bundle of nerves. Her hands shook, and she had dark circles under her eyes. I wanted to grab some stuff for her, toss her in my car, and take off to somewhere, anywhere she felt safe."

Matt shook his head and continued. "How could Dave either not see or not care about that? I was furious with him. I forgave him, but I'll never forget."

"Forget the fairy tale Dad told Dave. That stress caused Melissa's cancer. It killed her. Dave killed her, and the man who threatened Dave killed her," Matt said as a tear formed in the corner of his eye.

"What time did you leave White Bear Lake?" Martin asked.

"About 9:30."

"Where did you go from there?" Pete asked.

"To my office in Rosemount."

"What time did you arrive?" Pete asked.

"A little after 10:00."

"How did you find out Melissa was diagnosed with cancer?" Pete asked.

"She called me that night. She was a wreck. They were planning a family. She waited until Dave thought the time was right. She always wanted kids. She'd have been a great mom."

"The way my brain works," Pete said, "if I got a call like that, I'd remember the day and the hour she called. How about you, Matt? Does your mind work that way?"

Looking at his hands, not Pete, Matt shook his head and said, "I only remember it was midweek, and I was at work."

"You told us how you felt about Dave," Pete said, "but it was all about after Melissa died. How did you feel about him before the incident in downtown St. Paul that caused all the stress?"

"I liked him, but I didn't think he was good enough for Melissa. She was one of a kind, the kind of person who lit up a room. I think she could have done better, but she loved him, and he loved her. I guess that's the important thing. But he didn't love her enough to walk or run away, instead of testifying. Sorry. I know I sound like a broken record."

Matt logged into Linda's schedule and determined she should be home until 10:00 tomorrow morning, then after 4:00. "Even better than banker's hours." he rolled his eyes.

Pete and Martin got Linda's phone number, thanked Dave, went through the usual routine, and left for Lakeville.

Three family members down, three to go.

What are the chances Matt won't call Amy? Pete wondered. *And will she spend the next twenty minutes concocting her answers and arranging for someone to back up her story?*

SIXTEEN

Amy Campbell,
Dave's Sister-in-Law

"It's 9:10," Pete said as he and Martin walked back to the unmarked car. "One more stop and call it a day?"

"I thought we'd just gotten a good start, but I suppose you could sell me on that. I see you've fallen back into your old habits."

"Meaning?" Pete asked.

"Meaning, why let food interfere when we're on a mission?"

"But Martin, you had a Diet Coke just an hour ago."

"And I'm amazed it didn't fill me to the brim."

"In that case, what do you say? Want a granola bar ... or two, or hope we pass someplace where we can pick up something between here and Lakeville?"

"Let's gamble," Martin said. "If we don't find something, at least we have a console full of granola bars."

They took I-35 past the Buck Hill ski area to Lakeville. "Katie and I have spent a lot of wonderful hours there," Pete said, referring to Buck Hill.

"The way you say that, it sounds like never again. Is that the case?"

"Definitely not. In fact, I'm wondering how old Teddy has to be before we can take him skiing for the first time."

"I'd think any time after eighteen would be safe," Martin said.

"The good news is, if it takes that long, he can spend the last few years at home babysitting himself and his siblings, while Katie and I ski."

"You'd make him do that? I'm shocked!"

"By the time he reaches sixteen, he'll probably prefer that to skiing with a couple of old duffers." Pete smiled.

"You, maybe, but I'll bet he never refers to Katie that way." Martin laughed.

They passed a few places where they could have gotten food but resorted to the granola bars to keep from arriving at the Campbell's unreasonably late. After all, this wasn't an emergency.

Dave's sister-in-law Amy Campbell and her husband Robert lived in a large, two-story, cream-colored craftsman style home with a forest-green front door and shutters. A three-stall garage occupied the left side. The two-story, enclosed entry was a two-tone brown brick, as was the bottom three feet of the house. A Palladium window above the front door adorned the entry. To the right of the entry was a four-pane window with a Colonial-style grid system.

This large house, like the others in the neighborhood, took up most of the quarter-acre lot on which it was built. It appeared to be another case where the trees were mowed down to hasten the construction of homes. A white, six-foot-tall privacy fence separated their home from those on either side, perhaps compensating for the closeness.

Once again, interior lights sparked Pete and Martin's optimism about finding someone home. After parking down the road, they hurried to the front door, anxious to complete their last interview of the day.

A woman who appeared to be in her mid-forties answered the doorbell and asked through the screen door who they were and what they wanted at this hour.

I'd be shocked if she hasn't been told by her parents or brother or both to expect us, Pete thought. *And I'm glad we didn't stop to get something to eat.*

He and Martin produced their badges and IDs and asked if she was Amy. When she nodded, Pete said, "We have some questions for you and your husband."

"Robby isn't here. He flew to Phoenix this morning."

"What time did he leave?" Pete asked.

"If you're asking what time he walked out the door, I don't know. I was still asleep. If you're asking the time he flew out, I don't know that either. He only told me what time he'd get home, since it's all that really matters to me."

"Why did he fly to Phoenix?" Pete asked.

"For work."

"When are you expecting him back?" Pete asked.

"Tomorrow. He said he'd be here in time for dinner."

"And what time is that?" Martin asked.

"He meant 7:00, but he's often late. I never have dinner ready until 7:30 or 8:00, to keep it from ending up overcooked. So it's possible he meant 7:30 or 8:00."

Crossing her arms and frowning, she continued, "You said you had some questions for Robby and me. What kind of questions?"

"You heard about your brother-in-law David?" Pete asked.

"Of course. I don't live in a hermetically sealed chamber." She motioned to the space around her.

"We're looking for any information we can get about him to help with our investigation," Martin said.

"I'm certain I can't provide anything you haven't already gotten from Mom, Dad, and Matt."

"We'd appreciate your cooperation," Martin said. "It shouldn't take long. And the sooner we begin ..."

"Yeah, yeah," she interrupted. "Come in," she said, unlocking the screen door.

Amy Campbell was a petite five foot four with auburn hair, a reddened nose with a prominent bridge, and a small mouth. Her green eyes were red and puffy. She wore gray sweats and white sneakers.

After motioning them to follow, she led them through the foyer and into an office. As they entered that room, they noticed large picture windows to the right. To the left was a wide opening into the living room.

In front of the office windows sat a round table covered with swatches of a variety of fabrics. Straight ahead was a desk and a high-backed, ergonomic leather chair. Bookshelves lined the wall behind the desk, and two Scandinavian-style armed chairs faced it.

They continued on into the living room. Straight ahead were picture windows opening into the back yard. The wall to their right was slate gray and had a white fireplace with a honey-oak mantle and a Clerestory window on each side. Facing the fireplace and the picture windows was a light-gray, leather, L-shaped sofa with an ottoman. Black and dark-gray, herringbone-pattern oversized chairs stood with their backs to the picture windows.

"Have a seat," she said, leaving the choice to them.

After Pete and Martin selected the herringbone chairs, Amy slumped in the sofa, facing them. "Okay, let's get this over with," she said. "It's been a horrible day, and all I want to do is get in bed, hoping I can escape into dreams."

"You're referring to Dave?" Pete asked.

"Of course," she sighed. "I can't believe someone killed him. He was a good, honest, and caring person. It's too crazy for words."

"How did you find out?" Pete asked.

"Matt's wife Linda called. I was tied up all day with a project, working to meet the deadline. It's been more of a challenge this time, because the people keep changing their minds."

"What kind of project?" Pete asked. "What kind of work do you do?"

"I'm an interior designer," she sighed, like talking required more energy than she could muster.

Gesturing around the living room, Martin asked, "Am I correct in assuming you designed the furnishings in your home?"

Amy nodded.

"I like your taste and selections," Martin said. "I wish we could afford to work with you. Our home sorely needs updating."

"The job of an interior designer is to help you determine the budget and work within those constraints," she said. Her voice and her face were both free of emotion.

"When did you last see David?" Martin asked.

"Two weeks ago tomorrow. I tried to meet him for lunch at least once every couple of weeks. On the days we planned to meet, I scheduled the rest of my day around our lunches. We were supposed to get together

Friday. It would have been Melissa's fortieth birthday, and I didn't want him to spend the day alone, without moral support or comfort."

Her eyes grew moist, then the tears began streaming down her cheeks. She blotted them with a sleeve.

Then she continued, through sobs, "Robby got angry with me when I included Dave in everything after Melissa passed. He wanted more time for just the two of us. If I didn't know better, I'd have thought he was jealous."

"Did your husband know about those lunches?" Pete asked.

She sniffed and said, "Of course not. He wouldn't have liked it."

"Who paid?" Pete asked.

"I insisted that we take turns."

"With a credit card?" Pete asked.

Amy nodded.

"Does your husband see those statements?" Pete asked.

"So he'd have discovered it that way? No, I have my own credit cards, due to my business. He doesn't' see those statements. I don't get paper statements, and he doesn't know my passwords."

"Do you have any children?" Martin asked.

"Just Robby. Much as I wanted at least a half dozen, I changed my mind when I realized he'd have found them threatening. And he'd have hated the time they required. He confirmed my suspicions when he got so jealous about me including Dave after Melissa died."

"Do you know who Dave's friends and enemies were?" Martin asked.

"I know Melissa was his best friend, and he was lost after she died. They did everything together. Other than

Matt, Linda, and me, I didn't know any of his other friends. And enemies? I don't know of any." Pausing, she said, "Well, except for the guy he testified against. It makes sense he'd be an enemy. After all, he lost I think it was a decade of his life, and Dave might have been the biggest reason ... except for the guy's stupidity, I mean."

She mentioned Matt, even though Matt blames Melissa's death on him," Pete thought, *and she mentioned Matt's wife. It's interesting she didn't mention her husband.*

"Tell us about your husband," he said.

"He works in Honeywell's aerospace division in Golden Valley. He's an engineer."

She described David the person, and her husband by his career, Pete thought and pondered the significance.

"What do you drive these days?" Pete asked.

"A Lexus RX. It's important I make the right impression with my clients and potential clients." She shrugged and sniffed.

"Does color matter?" Pete asked.

"I don't think so. It's white."

"How about your husband?" Pete asked, waiting for her to challenge his need to know.

"Robby's assigned a company car. It's a white Honda Pilot."

"You had lunch with David the week before last, correct?" Martin asked.

Amy nodded.

"Did he seem more anxious or nervous that day?" Martin asked.

"He knew the release date for the man he testified against was rapidly approaching, and he dreaded it. He worried the guy might decide or have already decided to get even." Amy wiped away the nonstop tears with the heels of her hands.

SEVENTEEN
The Autopsy

Pete arrived home at 10:30. That was early for the first night after being assigned a new case. It was too late to spend time with Teddy, now that he slept through the night. It didn't stop Pete from standing alongside the crib, looking down at his son ... and anxiously awaiting the next time he could rock him to sleep.

It wasn't too late to hold Katie in his arms, take in her sweet smell, and feel blessed. She loved to hear about his work, and he shared the details he could, leaving out the names.

"They killed him with a paver?" she asked. "Is this a first for you?"

"Yes, but the outcome is the same ... just not as messy as many."

"As long as you aren't the medical examiner, anyway?"

"Right, and the autopsy is on the agenda for tomorrow."

Katie plugged her nose.

Pete smiled and said, "If I didn't know better, I'd think you'd witnessed one."

They fell asleep that night in the favorite position for both of them. Katie had her head on Pete's chest, and Pete's right arm was around her shoulders.

Thursday morning, Martin didn't sit on his thumbs, while Pete was at David Barrett's autopsy. He arrived at Gordon Shevlin's office at 7:50 on Thursday morning and waited for the person assigned to the front desk to arrive. That happened at 7:58.

After learning the same person opened up at that position the day before, Martin asked him to find a substitute so they could talk. Five minutes later, Martin and Jim were strolling outside, enjoying another unusually warm September morning.

Jim hadn't seen Gordon arrive or leave their offices yesterday morning between 7:58 or so, the time he reached the front desk, and the critical time, 8:30. He confirmed that aside from the emergency exit, the only way to get in and out was by passing the front desk where he sat, and he didn't think anyone passed unbeknownst to him.

After they returned to the offices, Martin requested that Jim page Gordon, asking him to come to the front desk. When Gordon arrived, Martin told him to find the two friends who knew what time he arrived yesterday and have them come to the front desk, one at a time.

Martin met with them individually. Both supported Gordon's alibi, saying he was there between 7:55 and 8:30 yesterday morning. And they did this both before and after they were told that lying about it could make them accomplices, punishable with time in prison.

He finished up at St. Paul Public Works and reached headquarters at 8:45. Figuring he had at least another thirty minutes before Pete left the ME's office, he called Matt Peterson's wife Linda, hoping to schedule a meeting. Linda was on the way to her next appointment and had to wait until she arrived to check her schedule. She said she'd call back shortly.

Five minutes later, Linda called and wanted to know how much time they'd need.

Martin said it shouldn't take more than thirty minutes, and probably not that long. He offered to meet her wherever it would work best for her.

"It'll work best if you wait until I get home. It's an early day, and I'll be there by 4:00."

"Can you swing anything earlier?" he asked.

"Not readily."

"Okay. If that changes, please let me know."

She ended, saying, "I was so sorry to hear about poor Dave."

Martin was in the process of looking up Joel Milroy's phone number when Pete walked in.

"Could Michelle lift a five-and-a-half or six-pound paving brick and bring it down with enough force to fracture someone's skull?" Pete asked.

"Good morning to you too, Pete. And yes, she not only carries boxes of canned foods we buy at Costco down the stairs to the basement, she also lifts them and puts them on shelves higher than she is tall. Plus she works out at least five days a week, including exercises with a five-pound weight in each hand. Keep in mind, once you had the paver up, over your head, gravity would help to provide lots of downward force."

Pete nodded and said, "That's also true for Katie. Teddy weighs about eighteen pounds, and she lifts him up over her head no sweat. Add a large dose of adrenaline and ... So which one did it?"

"Huh?" Martin looked confused.

"Who is guilty of this one, Michelle or Katie?"

Martin smiled and said, "Next time I talk to Katie, I'll tell her she's a suspect. Do you think you should seize her passport and her car keys?"

"What do you think, Martin?"

"I think this discussion is about the autopsy, not the Amazons we married." Martin chuckled. "What did they find?"

"David Barrett died of a TBI, a traumatic brain injury," Pete said. "In his hair, they found small fragments of a dark-gray cement and a bit of dirt. Both were sent to Forensics to check for a match with the fragments of a paver and the dirt found on his garage floor and near his body. The blows to his head fractured his skull, and they found bone fragments lodged in his brain. Based on the extent of the injuries and the damage to the brain stem, he died instantly."

Martin asked, "Does killing someone with a paving brick require more or less anger or hatred than doing it with a gun?"

"Since it's up close and personal, it seems like more, doesn't it? However, he was hit from behind, so they didn't have to look at his face. That's unfortunate. They might not have been able to do it while looking at his face."

"That didn't stop Cameron Remer from attempting to beat him to a pulp."

"Good point. By the way, Martin, he looked a lot like his brothers."

Martin told Pete about his meetings at Gordon Shevlin's office and the meeting he'd scheduled with Linda Peterson. "I tried to schedule it for earlier, but this way we'll meet at her home ... and we might be able to speak with one or both of her daughters. I was about to call Joel Milroy when you interrupted."

"Busy morning, Martin. It sounds like working with me is holding you back."

"For sure, but your bubbly personality makes it worth the sacrifice." Martin laughed.

"Let's hold off on Milroy for a bit and call the guy Matt Peterson said he met with yesterday morning. Then we'll check with Forensics about the contacts on Barrett's cellphone and computer."

EIGHTEEN

Jerry Donnelly and Forensics

"We'll review Barrett's contact information over lunch?" Martin smiled.

"If I didn't know better, Martin, I'd think that was some kind of snide reference to yesterday's meal schedule." Pete laughed.

"Yesterday's meal schedule?" Martin rolled his eyes. "You mean yesterday's decision to resort to granola bars in lieu of a meal?"

"Admit it, Martin. You're happy with what we accomplished by doing that."

"Well," Martin drew the word out, "yes, I am."

"I promise to try to do better today," Pete said. "Did you have to tighten your belt this morning?"

"Tighten it? I had to punch a new hole to keep my slacks from dropping to the floor." Martin gazed skyward.

Pete punched in Jerry Donnelly's phone number and put the call on speaker. Both he and Martin smiled when Donnelly answered. Pete identified himself and told Donnelly he was on speaker, so his partner, Martin Tierney, could participate.

"I don't get it," Donnelly said. "Why do you want to talk to me? I haven't been speeding, robbed a bank, or beat my wife."

Initially, he also claimed that he didn't meet with Matt Peterson yesterday.

"Okay, I'm making a note of that," Pete said. "Be prepared to testify under oath to it."

"Hang on a second," Donnelly said. "Let me double check my schedule. Several seconds later, probably the length of time Donnelly thought reasonable to do so, he said, "My mistake. It doesn't seem like yesterday. I've been so busy, this week seems like one long day."

"Where did you meet and at what time?" Pete asked.

"My schedule says Café Cravings at 8:30."

"What time did Peterson arrive?" Pete asked.

"All I know is, he was there when I arrived a few minutes early."

"Did he seem nervous or rattled?" Pete asked.

"I have no idea. I was too nervous and rattled to notice."

"How was he dressed?" Martin asked.

"Slacks and a navy-blue shirt. No tie or suitcoat."

"Did he look rumpled?" Martin asked.

"Not that I noticed, but I wasn't paying attention to those things."

"Did you shake hands?" Martin asked.

"Of course."

"Was his hand scuffed or were his fingernails dirty or chewed up?" Martin asked.

"His handshake felt firm and confident. That's all I remember. So, what has he done?"

Pete and Martin thanked him and walked over to the Forensics Services Unit.

They learned the analysis wasn't yet complete, but the cement fragments removed from Barrett's hair and the wound to his head were almost certainly of the same material as the fragments of a paver found in the garage, as well as those around the Barrett foliage. Also, the bits of dirt matched the dirt in the hole created when someone extracted one of those pavers ... possibly providing the murder weapon. Unfortunately, they hadn't found the rest of that paver, which might have contained a wealth of trace evidence, including skin or fibers from the attacker. Thus far, they had no other trace evidence.

Thanks to the suggestions provided by Brian and Jack Barrett, they'd quickly accessed Dave's cellphone and home computer. They handed Pete a page showing all of Dave's incoming and outgoing phone calls and voicemail messages for the last two weeks, as well as a printout of all incoming and outgoing text messages. They wondered if the person who attacked Dave contacted him during that time frame. They felt confident Edgar Waltham hadn't. They also got a printout of his contacts and their contact information, as well as a printout of his list of clients.

"Hitting someone over the head with this stack of pages could prove fatal," Pete told Martin on the way back to his office.

Once there, they began checking all of Barrett's incoming and outgoing calls for yesterday. They saw the call his brother Jack mentioned and a second from him about ten minutes later.

Checking calls for the last two weeks, they saw Dave had spoken with Tim and/or Dorothy Peterson and Amy Campbell, and both Brian and Jack, but no other family members. Of particular interest was his call to his friend, Mike Hinckley, on Tuesday night. It lasted fifty-three minutes.

Then they split up the text and voicemail messages, scanning for anything that seemed antagonistic or threatening. Turned out there was nothing more threatening than, "If you don't call back before 3:00, I'm cancelling my appointment." That was an incoming message from someone whose name also appeared on the list of clients on his computer.

Before taking off for lunch, they called and texted Edgar Waltham's son Zachary, hoping.

Trying to be optimistic, they left both a voice and text message. Then they called Edgar's cell. As anticipated, their call went straight to voicemail. They left a message, asking Edgar to notify Zachary to return their call and/or text.

"Before lunch," Martin said, "how about trying to reach Barrett's friend one more time, now that we have the correct phone number? I'm particularly interested in what he and Barrett talked about for almost an hour the night before Barrett was murdered."

"When it comes to lunch," Pete said, "what'll it be? Granola bars, omelets, salads, or who knows?"

"Let's do granola bars," Martin said. "I hate to break with tradition."

"Grab your suitcoat. We'll start a new tradition. Keys Café or?"

"Willing to spend fifteen or twenty minutes driving each way?"

"Sure, as long as you can order and eat in under thirty minutes." Pete chuckled. "What do you have in mind?"

"Lucky's 13 Pub has terrific cobb salads, and you'll love their ranch dressing. Michelle and I went there with some friends. There's one in Roseville and another in Mendota. Distance-wise, could be a horse apiece."

"I have a proposal, Martin. It's 3:00. What would you think about having lunch at the Mendota location, but delaying lunch long enough to call Dave's friend Mike Hinckley and Dave's attorney Joel Milroy?"

"I'm anxious to speak with Hinckley. Did Barrett tell him something that will point us in the right direction? By the way, Pete, are you planning to stick your neck out when it comes to Edgar Waltham?"

"I'm trying to determine the best way to do that."

NINETEEN
Mike Hinckley, Dave's Friend

Before proceeding with their new plan, Martin called Linda Peterson to get her okay with a new arrival time of about 6:30.

She said it would work much better for her and thanked him for the advance notice.

Then Pete dialed the number David Barrett had for Mike Hinckley, hoping. He held his breath, waiting for Mike to answer. The phone rang four times before his call entered the vast void known as voicemail. Remaining optimistic, Pete left a message. He explained who he was, said he was calling about David Barrett, and requested a return call ASAP. He didn't mention Dave's murder.

Disconnecting, he sighed and said, "The best laid plans ..." Then he located Milroy's phone number, hoping to hear from Hinckley while they ate or at least before they met with Linda Peterson.

Hinckley didn't give him a chance to call Milroy.

Pete's phone vibrated, and the screen showed a 301 area code. Maryland. He smiled and said "Culnane."

"You just called me?" a deep, anxiety-ridden voice asked. "I just tried calling Dave, and my call went right to voicemail. Why did you call? Is Dave okay? A call from the police is freaking me out."

126

"First, I have to tell you that you're on speaker, and my partner Martin Tierney, is here with me. Then, I regret to inform you ..."

"No!" Mike interrupted. "You can't be calling to tell me he's dead. Please, he's in the hospital, but he's still alive and wants to see me, right?"

"No," Pete said. "Someone attacked him yesterday morning in his garage. He died instantly. I'm calling because his brothers said the two of you were good friends. Forensics retrieved his phone call records, and I see you spoke with him the night before he died. He might have said something that will help with our investigation. In addition to notifying you of his death and expressing our sympathy, that's why I'm calling. I would have notified you yesterday, in light of your close connection with the victim, but we just obtained your phone number."

"Oh Lord," a shaky voice replied. "He called me about 11:30. He knew I'm always up until midnight. He was exhausted, but couldn't sleep. He needed to talk. He was scared. He felt like at least two threats competed to see which got to him first. He told me about the release of the man he'd helped convict of armed robbery, and he told me about being attacked that evening on the way to his car. He feared at least one other person could be joining the lineup. Just before leaving work that evening, he called the president of a company and reported his suspicions that the treasurer had embezzle significant sums. He never thought becoming a CPA required a bodyguard, flak jacket, or hazardous duty pay. He wanted to know what happened to the kinder, gentler world we grew up in."

"Did he give you the name of the man he reported the embezzling to?" Pete asked, pen in hand and notepad at the ready.

"No. He just said it was a local, small company."

No problem, Pete thought. *We know all the phone numbers he called Tuesday and the times.*

"I had trouble understanding him," Mike said, "and, I'm ashamed to admit, I asked if he'd resorted to alcohol as a coping mechanism. I felt like a first class jerk when he told me the guy who attacked him that night knocked out his front teeth."

"I apologized profusely," Mike continued, " and he laughed. He told me I was part of an exclusive club. Brian and Jack drew the same conclusion."

"Did the guy who knocked out his front teeth utter any additional threats?" Pete asked. "Did Dave say anything about that?"

"Dave understood that someone would be upset about an IRS audit, but not enough to knock out his front teeth and threaten worse. He wondered what to expect next. Dave has always been a calm, self-assured guy. He sounded like anything but, when he called on Tuesday."

"Then Dave's voice grew calmer, and he began reminiscing about 'the good old days.' He talked about our college days and about Melissa. He said how much he missed her. He chuckled and said that, for a while that evening, he thought he might be joining her. Then he said something that hit me like a blow to the gut. He said, 'You know, Mike, that wouldn't be all bad.' I told him he still had a lot of living to do, and we still had a lot of good times together ahead of us."

"He apologized for calling so late. Said he'd hoped a friendly voice would help him relax ... and it did. He sounded a lot better before he disconnected."

"I blew it!" Mike exploded. "Instead of helping him relax, I should have told him to pack a bag and get on the next flight to Maryland ... to get out of there immediately. How could I be so stupid?!"

Pete and Martin heard a sniff combined with a deep sigh.

"You did him a huge favor," Pete said. "You were there for him when he needed you. There was no way of knowing he'd be attacked the next morning. His brothers had no idea, and they were with him earlier that night."

"Let's return to the guy he helped convict," Pete said. "Did the two of you talk about that case back then or Tuesday night? Specifically, I'm wondering how convinced he was they had the right guy."

"I assume he was positive. Knowing Dave the way I do, he would never testify against him otherwise."

"I saw in his testimony that he described the way that person was dressed," Pete said. "Did he talk about seeing his face?"

"No, but he had to have seen it, didn't he?"

"It would seem so," Pete said, "but a person can look radically different from two different angles."

"Are you saying he screwed up?"

"No, Mike, I'm not," Pete said. "I'm less certain the courts didn't. Dave did everything he could to make St. Paul safer, and he's to be commended for that. Thanks for your help, Mike."

TWENTY
Joel Milroy, Dave's Attorney

Drained by their conversation with Mike Hinckley, Pete and Martin took a break before calling Joel Milroy. Pete plugged the vending machine and returned with two Diet Cokes and a couple of bags of peanuts. "Sorry, Martin," he said, "lunch succumbed to an early dinner."

"There's a time for every purpose," Martin said. "A time to eat, a time to call, a time to drive, a time to question, a time to challenge, a time to accept, a time to reject, a time to Mirandize, a time to arrest. Need I say more?"

"No," Pete laughed. "I think you've pretty well covered our job descriptions."

He put his phone on speaker to include Martin in the conversation with Dave Barrett's attorney during the trial that convicted Edgar Waltham.

"Why was Dave so certain Waltham was the person who attacked the woman in the Golden Rule Building?" Pete asked Milroy. "Did he see his face?"

"He didn't get a good look at Waltham's face, but he described him to a T, from his sweatshirt, to his pants, and baseball cap. The icing on the cake was when Waltham had a gun on him."

"What did Dave say about the attacker's face?"

130

"Nothing that I remember, but he got a better look at the clothes ... and the gun, of course."

"Did he describe the gun?" Pete asked.

"No, he just said he had a gun."

"Did he attempt to work with a sketch artist?" Pete asked.

"He tried, but the artist threw up his hands and gave up, because Dave gave him so little to go on."

"Yesterday," Pete said, "we located another eyewitness, and she described the attacker's face. She said he had a rose-colored birthmark on the right side of his face. Did Dave say anything about that?"

"I don't know that he saw the right side of his face. He may have only seen the left side. Why didn't the person you spoke with come forward before or during the trial?" Joel sounded exasperated.

"She was rushing for the airport and called 911," Pete said. "By the time she returned, the trial was over and it never occurred to her to ask about it."

"Did she mention the birthmark during her 911 call?" Milroy asked.

"She thinks she did, but isn't positive," Pete said. "She was stressed out at the time."

"How confident are you that she's reliable?"

Pete explained, "She described the whole thing, including where the attack occurred and where Dave was. I had nothing to do with the case, but she's certainly believable."

"Lovely! And what do you intend to do about this?"

"How about the victim?" Pete asked. "Did she see her attacker?"

"She said she didn't, so she didn't testify. And again, what do you intend to do?"

"Did they find her purse?" Martin asked.

"No."

"Were any of her credit cards used?" Martin asked.

"She didn't carry credit cards or any kind of ID. She had a change purse with cash in it. If someone found the purse, there was no way to return it. Now answer my question. What are you planning to do?"

"Provide the information to the county attorney and the appropriate people in our department," Pete said.

"And?" Milroy asked.

"If the wrong person was convicted, I hope they'll do whatever it takes to exonerate him. It's cost him ten years of his life and now, due to his record, he's unable to return to work in his chosen field."

"Tell us about Waltham's threats," Martin said.

"What do you want to know?"

"What form did they take?" Martin asked.

"There were a few typed notes, and a couple of calls to Dave's home."

"Did Forensics find any fingerprints on the notes?" Martin asked.

"No."

"Do you have copies of them?" Pete asked.

"Yes."

"How long would it take to retrieve them?" Pete asked.

"Five or ten minutes."

Joel called back when he had the notes and transcribed documentation of the phone calls in front of him.

The notes were all some variation of "You can't testify I attacked that woman. I didn't! Please don't force me to keep you from doing this. I'm innocent, and I can't permit you to destroy me and my family! Protect yourself and your family. Refuse to testify!"

The wording of the telephone calls was similar and no more nor less threatening.

"If Waltham didn't do it," Milroy said, "why the threats? I think they helped get him convicted. They may have been the proverbial icing on the cake."

Twenty-One
Dinner and
Linda Peterson, Dave's Wife's
Sister-in-Law

The good news was, Pete and Martin wrapped up their contacts with Hinckley and Milroy before they left for dinner. The bad news was, that put them in the height of rush hour traffic.

Pete multitasked on the way to Lucky's 13 Pub in Mendota. He called Edgar Waltham, who didn't answer. Nor did his son Zach or his ex-wife Sandra. "At least I'm consistent," he told Martin as he slid his phone into a pocket.

He brought along the list of calls from Dave Barrett's cellphone and checked to see whom he may have called about an embezzling company treasurer. If he made that call just before leaving work on Tuesday, it looked like the company president must have been Gregory Elko.

He shared the news with Martin and said, "Later. Wondering how much we can accomplish yet today, if we succeed or fail in meeting with Robert Campbell, Dave's brother-in-law."

"For sure. There's still so much on the list. For starters, in addition to Waltham's son and ex-wife, we've got Barrett's neighbors. Too bad much of Barrett's family lives so far from St. Paul."

"There's always tomorrow." Pete smiled.

The crowd beat them to Lucky's 13 Pub, but they found a table off to the side. Both men ordered the cobb salad with ranch dressing that Martin recommended. He failed to mention that one would have fed both of them. They hoped the leftovers would survive several hours in the trunk. The clouds that moved in a few hours ago would help. So would the rapidly approaching sunset.

"We could always ask Linda if she has a cooler and an ice pack we can borrow," Martin said.

"Are you suggesting we ask before or after we start the interview?"

"Yes." Martin laughed.

"A tall, slender woman with mocha-colored skin, long black hair, and beautiful dark-brown eyes answered the door. She appeared to be in her early- to mid-forties and wore blue jeans, a pink top, and sneakers. "Martin?" she asked through the screen.

When he nodded, she said, "Come in. I'm Linda, and I'm so glad you delayed your arrival. It gave us plenty of time to eat dinner and clean up. Now I won't be a nervous wreck."

Pete and Martin noticed that pleasant smells suggesting hamburgers, fried onions, and French fries lingered.

She took them to the family room where they'd interviewed her husband. Again Pete and Martin sat in the oversized chairs and, like her husband, she sat on the sofa.

"I can't believe what happened to Dave," she said before Pete or Martin had a chance to ask a question. "I guess you already know that Matt called me as soon as he found out. He was pretty rattled. I also heard what happened to Dave the night before. What's going on? He was such a good person. I just wish he hadn't gotten involved in that trial ten years ago. Is all this the result of that? Maybe he shouldn't have been so noble. If he hadn't been, he'd probably be alive right now." She frowned.

"Where are Matt and your daughters?" Pete asked, wondering if he lurked in another room, listening and influencing Linda's answers.

"He took them to the mall to keep them out of our hair. They're still in shock about Dave. Several times today, Clare broke into tears and couldn't stop crying. She's an emotional kid. They both dearly loved Dave, and his absence is sure to leave a hole in their lives."

"Did Dave get the cold shoulder from some members of Melissa's family after her death?" Martin asked.

"Initially, but I don't think that's been true for at least several months."

Martin asked, "How well did you know Dave?"

"I know he and Melissa meant the world to each other, and losing her almost destroyed him. I know both he and Melissa believed in and trusted God throughout her illness, and he continued after she died. I know he used alcohol to cope with her death, but with the help of AA was beating the need. I know he preferred chinos or jeans and sweatshirts or polos to suits. I know he loved my girls, and Tim and Dorothy. I know Tim and Dorothy loved him like a son, but don't tell Matt I said that. I know his favorite cookie was chocolate chip, and he liked devil's food cake with white frosting best. I don't know why anyone would murder him."

"Did you ever see him in a touchy situation or did he ever mention anyone he had trouble with?" Martin asked.

"I know Rob sometimes got irritated with him, but I think that was more Amy's doing than Dave's. I'm not sure she ever got over the crush she had on Dave. Don't get me wrong. She'd never have come between Melissa and Dave. She just never stopped thinking he was a cut above."

"Does she think Rob is 'a cut above?'" Martin asked.

"I'm sure she does," Linda said unconvincingly. "And I know he'd never hurt Dave. If you want my opinion, it had to be the guy he testified against. I heard he just got out of prison. I don't believe in coincidences." She shook her head.

"Did Dave talk about his friends or mention anyone he worried about meeting in a dark alley?" Martin asked.

"He never talked about his friends, and I can't believe he was afraid someone might be after him. He always seemed calm and relaxed when he met with my family and me."

Pete and Martin thanked Linda and gave her their business cards. They left before Matt and their daughters returned, but figured the girls were unlikely to add anything of value. Besides, they still had several stops before they ended their day.

Back in the unmarked car, Pete pulled out his phone, checking to see why it had vibrated.

Twenty-Two
Robert Campbell, Dave's Wife's Brother in Law

Edgar Waltham left a voicemail. *If I believed in old wives tales,* Pete thought, *I might wonder if his ears were burning, telling him someone was talking about him.*

The voicemail said, "Zach is here with me and Elaine. How about talking to him before he leaves? He'll be here until 11:00. We hope that works for you. Please call."

Pete called Edgar, contemplating the possible reasons for that request. He explained that he and Martin spent yesterday and today interviewing people. They'd like to meet with Zach tonight, but couldn't arrive until 10:00 or 10:30.

Edgar liked that. So it became the newest new plan.

Pete prioritized the meeting with Zach, because getting even for his dad's prison sentence and current problems could motivate an angry kid loyal to his dad. They also prioritized speaking with Dave Barrett's neighbors. Neither Brian nor Jack thought they could contribute anything, due to their schedules. But canvassing the neighbors was a standard police practice. It often produced information critical to solving the case. They might have seen someone scouting the neighborhood ahead of the attack or ...

Again Pete gazed longingly as they passed the Buck Hill ski area on their way from Burnsville to Lakeville. Best case, another two months separated him from the ski season. His and Katie's season ended early last year, due to her pregnancy. So it felt like forever since he rode a chairlift up and raced back down. He'd never consider trading Teddy for a season of skiing, but that didn't stop him from missing the sensation of the wind in his face and his skis reacting to his every move, each redistribution of his weight.

Forcing himself back into the present, he said, "Am I asking too much, Martin? It's going to be at least 10:30 or 11:00 by the time we wrap up tonight ... unless none of Barrett's neighbors are home. I'm happy to canvas his neighborhood and speak with Zachary alone, if you'd like to hang it up after we finish in Lakeville."

"And miss the chance to meet and interrogate a seventeen-year-old whose a sophomore in college? I'm thinking he could be an inspiration to Marty." Martin laughed.

"How is Marty doing in school?"

"He's doing okay, but he isn't particularly motivated. Michelle and I have tried to sell him on the benefits of concurrent enrollment, where he'd get college credit for some of his classes. I think Zachary must have done that. Marty's afraid that will take all the fun and free time out of high school."

Pete nodded and said, "Unfortunately, that sounds like a reasonable concern."

Robert Campbell answered the door. He stood six foot one and obviously spent a significant part of each week working out. He had curly, medium-brown hair, blue eyes, a prominent bridge on his long nose, and his thin lips might indicate their normal state or reflect his tight-lipped expression. He wore dress slacks, a white shirt with the sleeves rolled up to his elbows, and a striped tie pulled down from the open collar of his shirt.

After examining Pete and Martin's badges and IDs, he said, "Amy said you were looking for me. I hope you understand, after spending two long days between travel and meetings, I'm tired."

And you're home, but we won't reach our homes for at least another three hours, Martin thought.

When Robert continued standing there in the doorway, Pete said, "Mind if we come in?"

Robert sighed and said, "Fine, follow me." He led them to the office and the circular table in front of the windows.

Before asking any questions, Pete and Martin arranged their chairs, getting a straight on view of Robert's face. Then Pete said, "Amy told us you work in Honeywell's aerospace division. What does your division do?"

"A lot of research and development of things like aircraft engines, black boxes, navigation equipment, and on and on."

"How long have you been with Honeywell?" Pete asked.

"Twenty years. I was recruited right out of college, and I've grown with the company." He smiled.

"Your wife said you flew to Arizona," Martin said. "What's in Arizona?"

"I haven't told Amy. I'm afraid to. I know how she'll react. They're moving the aerospace division to Phoenix. I'm not sure she'll relocate, because all of her family is here."

"Any chance you could move to a different division?" Martin asked.

"I'd hate to do that. I like my team. Just the same, I'm looking into it." Rob sighed.

With that, Pete got down to business, asking, "What time did you fly out yesterday?"

Rob stiffened and asked, "What difference does that make?"

"Why are you afraid to say?" Pete asked.

"That's a stupid question!" Robert snarled. "I'm not afraid. My flight departed at 9:30."

"Was that the scheduled time or were you delayed?" Pete asked.

"That was the schedule."

"What time did you leave home?" Pete asked.

"At 6:00, and yes, I went right to the airport. I never know how long it'll take to get through TSA, and I had work I could do just as well at the airport as here or at my office."

"What airline?" Pete asked.

"United." Sweat moistened Rob's face as he asked, "Why the third degree?"

"Why so defensive?" Martin asked. "We're just gathering information, trying to determine whether you have an alibi. We ask everyone."

"Where did you park?" Martin asked.

"In the ramp, in long-term parking."

"What do you drive?" Martin asked, double checking.

"A Honda Pilot, and to save you having to ask, it's a 2018 and white. It's white platinum pearl, if that wasn't specific enough for you."

"Did you travel alone?" Martin asked.

Rob looked around, then whispered sarcastically, "No, I took my mistress." Returning to a normal voice, he said, "Yes, I traveled alone."

"How well did you know Dave?" Pete asked.

Rob's shoulders relaxed and he said, "Not well. I saw him at family functions, and Amy invited him over several times after Melissa died. We never hung around together. We didn't have any of the same friends or interests, other than family. And I don't think he ever picked up a golf club, went fishing, or cross country skied."

"When did you last see him?" Pete asked.

Rob rubbed his right cheek and stared at the table. Finally, he said, "You have to ask Amy. I don't know."

"Any idea who might have been angry with him or had a reason to hurt him?" Martin asked.

Rob shook his head.

"What do you wear when you travel, a suit or do you dress casually?" Martin asked.

"I usually wear a suit, but I went casual yesterday. I checked into the hotel before the meeting and had time to change."

"How do you define casual?" Pete asked, figuring that knowing this might come in handy.

Robert looked at him questioningly and said, "Chinos and a plaid shirt."

"I must have at least a half-dozen pairs of tan chinos," Pete lied, searching for more detail.

"Me too." Campbell smiled. "They're like my casual uniform."

"What time did you arrive at the airport?" Martin asked.

"I can't give you an exact time, but it was about 6:45?"

"And how long did it take you to get through TSA?" Martin asked.

"I have no idea."

"Was it fast or slow?" Martin asked.

"Faster than it often is, and slower than sometimes."

"Did you see anyone you know while in line or once you reached the gate?" Martin asked.

"No."

"In other words, you have no alibi for your whereabouts yesterday morning from 6:00 until 9:30?" Martin asked.

"Correct," Rob said. "I suppose that makes me a top suspect."

"Do you belong to the United Club?" Pete asked.

"I did. My membership expired, and I haven't gotten around to renewing it. I was kicking myself yesterday."

"We may have additional questions later," Pete said and obtained Robert's work and cellphone numbers.

He and Martin thanked Robert, gave him their business cards, and asked him to call if he thought of someone who had seen him somewhere in that time frame.

After they reached Martin's unmarked car, Pete said, "This is another case where I wish we had a search warrant and could check his house and car right now. Why would anyone voluntarily spend three hours hanging around the airport, especially if they didn't belong to the airline club? At least if you do, you have a more accommodating place to wait."

"I can imagine arriving at the airport earlier than necessary," Martin said. "I dread the additional time required, due to the security measures mandated after September 11. Perhaps Campbell is obsessive compulsive or paranoid? Maybe his transfer to Phoenix isn't assured. It will cost Honeywell tens of thousands of dollars to move him when you include moving costs, realtor fees, per diem, transportation, and on and on. They may be wondering whether he's worth it."

"So true, Martin. I'll call the airport police and find out how long TSA keeps the logs of boarding passes and IDs scanned by TSA. It won't prove what time he arrived at the airport. It will show what time he went through TSA. And why would he go to the airport and hang around ticketing or baggage claim?"

Pete didn't get the answer he'd hoped for. TSA only keeps those logs for 24 hours. In other words, he had to call at least eight hours ago. However, he also learned getting the information wouldn't have been straightforward. TSA would probably require a search warrant or subpoena. For now, they didn't have enough to justify either.

"Depending on what we discover today," Pete said, "reviewing the security camera closed circuit footage at the airport, looking for Robert Campbell's arrival time could be a priority due to the questionable times he gave us."

TWENTY-THREE
Dave's Neighbors

Pulling away from Campbell's house, Martin said, "We need to speak with Barrett's neighbors. Maybe one or more saw a white Honda Pilot. We also need to check out Zachary Waltham."

"True. Zachary strikes me as a strong prospect. After all, he demanded his mom take him to Stillwater to see his dad every couple of months. For a seven year old to do that, the attachment had to be strong and enduring."

"Or the seven-year-old loved to drive his mom crazy," Martin said. "I hope we're able to determine which shortly."

Due to the large lots in the vicinity of David Barrett's home and the lake across the street, Pete and Martin spoke only with the neighbors four homes north and south of his.

Pete started four homes north of Dave's and went south. Martin started four houses south of Dave's and worked his way north. Resident after resident supported Brian and Jack's conclusions that all of Dave's neighbors were at or on their way to work or school when he was attacked. Each time they thanked the resident and moved on, and the temptation grew to give up on this time-burner. Fortunately, they didn't.

Martin stood in front of his last door, waiting impatiently and trying to decide whether the living room lights were regulated by a timer and meant nothing. After ringing the doorbell a second time, he stood, counting down slowly from ten and preparing to descend the steps. That's when the entryway light came on. Through the door, a woman called out, "Who's there?"

Martin identified himself and, assuming she viewed him through the peephole in the door, he held up his badge and ID.

The woman said, "Okay," and opened the door. She wore a bathrobe and slippers, and she looked like she just woke up. Her brown, shoulder-length hair needed combing, and her glasses needed cleaning. Martin still displayed his badge and ID when Pete walked up and did likewise.

"I'm Denise Freeborn. Are you here about Dave?"

"Yes, ma'am," Martin said.

"What a tragedy," she said. "Dave and Melissa were lovely people and wonderful neighbors. I always thought this was a safe neighborhood. Not anymore. I hate the work that goes along with it, but I'm thinking about getting a German shepherd or a Doberman pinscher. I'd invite you in, but I don't want to pass on this bug. Do you mind if we talk through the screen door?"

They shook their heads, and Martin asked, "Any chance you were here between 6:00 and 9:00 yesterday morning?"

Denise nodded.

"Did you notice any activity in front of your home or Dave's?"

"I sure did! I've been fighting off this bug, staying home from work to keep from sharing it with my friends, and tired of being in bed. So for the last few days I've been in the living room, wrapped in a blanket, relaxing in my recliner, and reading a book. Both Tuesday and yesterday, I heard what sounded like an old wreck crawling past out front. Tuesday, this happened at about 7:00. Yesterday, it passed at about 7:20 or 7:30. I didn't pay that much attention to the times. I had no idea it might be important."

"Did you go to the window to check on the source of the racket?" Pete asked.

"Yes. It looked like an ancient red, Honda Civic."

"By any chance, did you get the license plate number?" Martin asked.

"No," she sighed. "It looked like a young kid, and I didn't want to complicate his life. I figured money must be tight or he wouldn't be driving a junker like that. You don't think he was involved in what happened to Dave, do you?"

"We hope to determine that," Pete said. "If perchance, you hear that car go past again, please try to get the license plate number."

She smiled, nodded, and said, "You bet!"

"Can you describe the noise it made?" Martin asked.

"Sure can. There was a loud ticking that sounded like a loose valve, and the kind of a whining made by a worn alternator, water pump, or steering pump."

Both men looked wide-eyed at her.

Denise chuckled and said, "My dad loved cars and did all the work on ours. Every time a neighbor had a problem, he solved it. I loved to watch, learn, and eventually help him."

"Can you provide that detailed a description of the driver?" Martin asked.

"Probably not. He was too young for me. He appeared to be about average height, and neither skinny nor plump. He wore a baseball cap, so I couldn't see much of his hair. The one thing I'm almost positive of is that it was a boy. However, in this day and age, I can't even be positive about that."

Pete and Martin thanked her and went through the routine with their business cards. Then they ran back to the unmarked car.

It was 9:10, and they wouldn't let Edgar know they'd be early. They wouldn't risk Zachary or Edgar developing an emergency requiring their immediate attention—elsewhere.

TWENTY-FOUR
Edgar Waltham, Again

En route to St. Paul's Frogtown neighborhood, Pete asked, "Has anyone ever hurt your dad so bad you wanted to kill them, Martin?"

Martin took his eyes off the road long enough to stare momentarily at the man he thought he knew so well.

"Murder, not just beat him to a pulp? It sounds like you have."

"No, but Dad has."

"You can't leave it at that. Tell me about it."

"My grandpa went into business with his best friend. The type of business doesn't really matter. What matters is, when they dissolved the partnership and split up the proceeds, the friend said my grandpa fixed the books and cheated him. Dad said his father was as honest as the day is long and would never dream of doing that. This guy made such a stink about it, my grandpa finally caved and gave him everything he wanted. The monetary loss made things tough for Grandma and Grandpa for about a year, but that wasn't what hurt Grandpa. Dad said the way his best friend treated him was devastating. Grandpa was six feet tall, and he got down to 140 pounds. Dad said he couldn't stand to see what the 'friend' did to his dad. He said, given the right opportunity, he could have killed that guy. Literally."

He went on, "Dad was seventeen at the time. The prefrontal cortex, the part of the brain that regulates impulse control and judgment, is still developing through the teen years and isn't fully developed until the mid-twenties."

"How do you know that?"

"I took some courses in psychology in college, including one in developmental psychology. I found that so interesting and important that I remembered it."

"Are you saying, based on that, if Zachary killed Barrett it's understandable?"

"His dad was pulled from his life when he was a young kid. Now he sees his dad continuing to struggle. Understandable? Yes. Acceptable to kill Barrett for that reason? *No.* That also applies to my dad. What I don't know is whether he'd have gone through with it, given the opportunity. I prefer to think the answer is no. I also think that experience made Dad into a better father."

"Because?" Martin asked.

"Because I always had jobs, responsibilities, and boundaries. I was held accountable when expectations weren't met. Failures in any of those areas resulted in the loss of privileges, such as being forbidden to go to a Twins game. I learned at an early age that there's a price to pay for allowing short-term goals to rule my life. In other words, for poor judgment."

"You're scaring me, Pete. Now I'm worried Marty's judgment might be lacking."

"And I'll spend most of Teddy's life wondering whether I'm a good parent. All I can tell you is, based on what I've seen and my dealings with Marty, you're doing well."

"Even so, I'm wishing we hadn't had this conversation." Martin groaned.

Reaching Frogtown, they hurried to the front door of Elaine Waltham's apartment building. Not waiting for an elevator, they ran up two flights of stairs.

Uncertain what kind of reception they'd get from Edgar, they returned to standing to the left and right of the apartment door while waiting for someone to respond to Martin's knock.

"Just a minute," Edgar called out, raising the suspense.

A minute later, the door was flung open by a kid wearing a St. Paul Saints baseball cap. It did a decent, but not a perfect job of hiding his eyes. Per his driver's license, he stood five feet ten and weighed 155. The hair that escaped the cap was dark brown, and his eyes were hazel. He stood there, looking at them until Pete said, "You must be Zachary."

"I prefer Zach."

"Okay, Zach," Pete said. "Is your dad here?"

"Yeah," he said, trying and failing to stare Pete down. "But I heard you want to talk to me."

"We want to talk to you and your dad," Pete said. "Please get him."

Zach closed the door in their faces.

Seconds later, Edgar opened it, looking embarrassed. "I thought you got everything you need from me," he said.

"A few more questions came up after we left yesterday. Find a place where my partner can meet with Zach, and another where I can meet with you."

"Martin and Zach can talk in my bedroom. You and I will meet in the living room," he said and waved them in.

151

"Zach, you heard me, right?" Edgar asked.

"Yeah, follow me," Zach told Martin.

When Pete heard the bedroom door close, he said, "If you were innocent, I don't understand why you sent threatening notes and made threatening phone calls to David Barrett before the trial. It seems like you wanted to be convicted."

Jumping to his feet, Edgar shouted, "You're right, it would have been stupid, and I *never* sent a single threatening note nor made a threatening phone call to David Barrett! I heard about it at the trial. It made no more sense to me then than it does now!"

Pete heard a door bang open, and the next thing he knew, Zach was in his face.

"That's not right!" he yelled. "Dad didn't do that."

A flustered Martin was on Zach's heels.

"And you know that because?" Pete asked calmly. "I heard Mom and Thad. They thought I was asleep, and I heard them mention Dad. So I got out of bed and stood by the door, listening. Mom said she wanted Thad to make a few pay phone calls and mail a few notes. She told him he couldn't lick the envelopes to seal them. He wanted to know how he'd seal them if he couldn't lick the flap. I wanted to scream, 'Use a damp sponge, you idiot!' I was only seven, but I knew that much." Zach rolled his eyes, then went on, "They fought. He didn't want to do it, but Mom put her foot down. I just realized the calls and notes were supposed to be threats that would get Dad convicted." Zach sighed and shook his head.

"How do you know they followed through?" Pete asked.

"I came home from school one afternoon and saw both of them sitting at the kitchen table, wearing the kind of gloves Mom sometimes brings home from work. They were sliding pages into envelopes. When they saw me, they both turned red and hurried to push everything together and into a manila envelope. I was supposed to be at soccer practice, but didn't feel like it. They were shocked to see me."

"Did you ever say anything to your mom about it?"

"No. I didn't understand."

"Thad is your mom's second husband?" Martin asked.

"Yes. What kind of a name is that?"

"Your last name is still Waltham," Martin said. "What's Thad's last name?"

"Norcross."

"Did he want to adopt you?" Martin asked.

"I don't think so. He never mentioned it. If he'd offered, I'd have said 'no way!' He's my dad." Zach said, pointing at Edgar. "I don't want anyone else."

Edgar sighed.

"Why would Thad go along with your mom's idea?" Martin asked.

"Because Mom always said it was her way or the highway. She told him there are all kinds of options out there."

"You're living with your mom and Thad?" Pete asked.

"Free room and board. Do you have any idea how much a dorm room and even the cheapest meal plan cost? And soon I'll need a different car. Plus, my little sister Wendy needs me."

Looking at Edgar, Martin asked, "Why would she do this?"

"I think she was still furious that I walked out when I found her with another guy. Sorry, Zach. You didn't need to hear that."

"You think I don't know? And she's still doing it."

Edgar stared at Zach, dumbfounded.

Pete and Martin responded similarly, but masked their reactions.

An eyewitness who said Edgar didn't do it, and now this, Pete thought. *How should we proceed when it appears to have nothing to do with our case?*

"What does your mom do for a living?" Martin asked.

"She's an RN at Regions."

"How about Thad?" Martin asked.

"He's a PCA, that's a personal care assistant. PCAs do all the things RNs hate to do." He laughed. "He's at Regions too. That's how they met."

"What shifts do they work?" Martin asked.

"Mom said she's clinging to rotating shifts. She's expecting to have to change to twelve-hour shifts anytime now. Right now, she's 7:00 a.m. until 3:00 p.m. Thad is always 7:00 p.m. until 7:00 a.m."

Although they'd just spent as much or more time questioning Zach as his dad, they were finished, for now, with Edgar.

Zach, on the other hand, was still in the crosshairs.

TWENTY-FIVE
Zach Waltham

"We have two options here," Pete told Edgar in front of Zach.

Edgar smiled, thinking he meant they could speak with Zach with or without him in the room. He was wrong. "We need to be alone with Zach while we speak with him. Do you prefer we do that here, in the living room, or in your bedroom?"

"Don't I have a parental right? He's a minor."

"Only if you don't attempt to influence his answers," Pete said. "It might not be easy, you know."

"I'm sure I know what you're thinking and ..."

Pete held up a hand, stopping him mid-sentence and said, "That's an example of what you can't say."

Edgar put his hands over his mouth and sat down.

Zach sat on the other end of the sofa.

Intelligent kid, Pete thought.

Knowing that reciting it now wouldn't help the situation, Pete held off on the Miranda warning and asked, "Where were you yesterday morning, between 6:00 and 9:00?"

Zach blew out a long, slow breath.

Buying time? Pete and Martin wondered.

After an extended pause, Zach said, "I was home until 7:00. Then I was out, driving around."

"Can you prove you were home until 7:00?" Pete asked.

"Mom was with me until 7:00."

"If she thought it would help you, I'll bet she'd say you were there, whether or not it was true," Pete said.

"I bet you could find a way to ask so she wouldn't know it was helping me."

"Then you drove around for two hours?" Martin asked.

Zach shrugged and said, "Well, no. Only for about an hour."

Martin said, "Where did you drive? Tell us your route and what you passed."

Zach stared at his hands, then took a deep breath, looked up and said, "I drove around Lake Phalen." The sweat rolled from his forehead and down one cheek.

"What streets?" Martin asked.

"Wheelock Parkway, Frost, Larpenteur, Arcade."

"Forgot an important one, didn't you?" Pete asked. "Why drive around Lake Phalen and bypass the street providing the best view?"

"Oh yeah, I forgot East Shore Drive."

"Where were you during that same time frame the day before?" Pete asked.

"Actually, pretty much the same area. I love that lake, and thought about parking and walking or running around it. But I didn't have enough time. I had to get going or I'd miss my first class."

"And you came to that sudden realization two days in a row?" Pete asked, eyebrows raised.

With a reddening face, Zach said, "I thought I'd left earlier yesterday. I was surprised to see how late it was as I neared the parking lot on East Shore Drive."

"Give us a more exact time when you were driving along East Shore Drive both days," Martin said.

Zach's sweat-soaked T-shirt made a soft suction-like sound as he pulled it away from his chest. He rearranged himself on the sofa before saying, "It was about 7:00 both days."

"Can anyone vouch for you any time between 7:00 and 9:00?" Martin asked. "Did you see anyone as you walked out to your car or while you were driving?"

Zach shook his head.

"You said your mom would say you were home between 6:00 and 7:00 both days. Now you say you were on East Shore Drive around 7:00," Martin said. "Which is it, Zach?"

"I guess Mom can only vouch for me between 6:00 and 6:45."

"You drove from home directly to East Short Drive?" Martin asked.

Zach nodded.

"I find it curious that the one street you forgot you traveled is the one you headed straight for when you left home." Martin said. "Why did you drive to East Shore Drive, Zach?"

"I was trying to calm down and relax. I had important tests both mornings, was up until early in the morning studying, and barely slept. I was afraid I was going to bomb the tests if I didn't get my nerves under control. Driving relaxes me."

Edgar looked every bit as uncomfortable as Zach, but he remained silent.

"What do you drive?" Pete asked.

"A 2000 red Honda Civic."

"Let's take a break and go check out your car, Zach," Pete said.

Zach smiled, stood, and said, "It's out in the lot."

Pete, Martin, and Edgar followed Zach out the door down the stairs and out to the parking lot.

Pete and Martin picked out his Honda before he got to it. It appeared in need of more than the engine work Denise mentioned.

"Here she is," Zach said, patting the hood.

"How about getting in, starting her, and putting her in gear?" Pete asked. "Then drive a lap around the parking lot."

Pete sighed as Zach began his trip around the lot. Denise was right. There was a loud ticking and a whining.

As soon as Zach returned, parked, and got out of his car, Pete said, "We have a problem, Zach. You admitted passing the location where David Barrett was murdered about the time it happened."

So Pete Mirandized him, while Zach stood open-mouthed, and Edgar went crazy.

As gently as possible, under the circumstances, Martin ushered Edgar to the far end of the parking lot. Then he blocked Edgar's return to Pete and Zach.

"I didn't do it," Zach stammered. "Yes, I drove by his house two days in a row, and yes, I was scouting it out, thinking about attacking him. But I wouldn't have killed him! And I realized yesterday as I drove past his home that attacking him wouldn't get Dad a job. It would only make things worse. Much worse. So I drove back home, then left for school about an hour later."

"Was your mom there when you got home?"

Zach shook his head.

"How about her husband?"

Again Zach shook his head and said, "I'm sorry. I know it was a stupid idea. I just wish I'd realized that last weekend, not yesterday."

"Did you see many cars as you drove along East Shore Drive?"

"Just a few."

"Can you describe any of them?"

"A Pilot. It made an impression, because it's a Honda. I'd love to have one."

"What color, Zach?"

"White."

"Any idea what time that was?" Pete asked.

"Best guess, around 7:20 or 7:30. I was about to or had just passed David Barrett's, before I headed home."

"I assume you know, thanks to the string of lies you told, we could arrest you tonight."

Zach stared at his feet and nodded.

"Since there's an ever-so-small chance I'm wrong about you," Pete held up his right hand with his index finger about a half inch from his thumb, "I'd hate to keep you out of your classes and force you to fall behind. If you promise to return all my phone calls and texts within ninety minutes, I'll let you go—for now. But trust me, if you don't do that, you'll give me no choice. And if you take off, I can guarantee we'll find you, no matter where you go."

"Yes, sir."

Then they walked over to Martin and Edgar.

Edgar looked ready to bite the head off the first thing that crossed his path, and Martin looked anxious to hang it up for the day.

It was 10:00 p.m., and Pete decided that was a good idea—for Martin's half of this team.

TWENTY-SIX
Closing Out Day Two

Martin dropped Pete and his leftover salad, which spent almost five hours in the trunk, off at headquarters at 10:20. After hearing the list of things Pete planned to accomplish, he reluctantly drove home.

Pete sprinted to his office. He had a lot to accomplish, and he hoped to achieve a large part of it tonight. He didn't think Commander Lincoln would be happy about it, but couldn't permit that to stop him.

First, he searched the Bureau of Criminal Apprehension (BCA) statewide image system, which contains mugshots from across Minnesota. Then he narrowed the search using SMT (scars, marks, tattoos), looking only for those with a birthmark on the cheek. Finally, he narrowed the search even further by looking only for those booked in the seven-county metro area between 2007 and 2019. There were only two matches.

He retrieved both mugshots. Only one person, Todd Trimont, had a rose-colored birthmark on his right cheek. The other man's birthmark, in addition to being on the wrong cheek, wasn't rose-colored.

The statewide imaging system showed Trimont was booked for armed robbery in 2008 and for second degree murder in 2010. Because the BCA's statewide image system is linked to the Criminal History System

160

(CHS), which the BCA also maintains, it took just one click for Pete to check Todd Trimont's convictions and prison terms. While the imaging system showed an arrest for armed assault in October of 2008, the CHS did not show a conviction.

I'll look that up later in the Minnesota Court Information System to determine why, Pete decided.

Setting that aside, he checked the CHS for Trimont's arrest in November of 2010. He discovered Trimont was convicted and sentenced to a prison term of forty years. In Minnesota, that meant twenty-six and two-third years in prison, and thirteen and one-third years on supervised release. Almost nine years of prison time down, and seventeen and a half to go. He wondered, *Would Trimont admit to the armed robbery in the Golden Rule Building since the statute of limitations ran out seven years ago? If not, did he brag to the other prisoners about putting one over on the cops, because someone else was convicted of his crime?*

He downloaded Trimont's photo and the one of the man with the wrong birthmark from the statewide imaging system. Then he went online and found photos of seven other men with rose-colored birthmarks on a cheek and built a photo lineup for Beth. He used only the photos of men who were or appeared to be within ten years of Trimont's age on his mug shot and at the time Beth witnessed the attack. All but two had the mark on the right cheek. Would Beth pick Trimont?

One down, two to go, he thought as he called Stephanie, the on-call county attorney. He explained the eyewitness description he obtained yesterday ruled out the person convicted of the 2009 armed assault in the Golden Rule Building. "I created a photo lineup to show that eyewitness the first chance I get," he told her.

He added, "Further complicating the situation, I just heard that the threats delivered to the eyewitness, in an effort to keep him from testifying, didn't come from Waltham, the person to whom they were attributed."

"Then who's responsible for them?" she asked.

"If what I was told is true, Waltham's ex-wife and her current husband. It sounds like she orchestrated it, in an effort to help insure her ex-husband's conviction. She may or may not have strong-armed her current husband into participating."

"Lovely. And you're telling me all this because?"

"If Edgar Waltham was wrongly convicted, I'd like to see justice done. I'd like to see him exonerated. He just completed his ten-year sentence. If he's innocent, in and of itself, that's a travesty. I'm not blaming anyone. But the system failed him. Prior to his conviction, he was a paramedic. An ex con is ineligible for work in that field or as an EMT."

Pete continued, "As soon as we disconnect, the next thing I'll do is write a supplemental report describing the eyewitness account, and forward it to the cold case unit and your office for review."

"In an effort to increase the likelihood that the powers that be look at and act upon this, I'd like to prove one other piece of the case was a fallacy, namely the threats to the eyewitness who testified at the trial. With some help from your office, I believe I can get a confession from the people who created and delivered those threats."

"What kind of help?"

"I don't believe either of them will confess without a plea bargain. And without their confessions, I doubt we'll ever prove it was them. She may demand a minimal or no sentence for both of them. I'm under the impression he'll do whatever she recommends."

"And why would she confess?" Stephanie asked.

"To protect her seventeen-year-old son. I plan to lead her to believe her confession is the only way to keep him out of jail. I assume you'll have to discuss this with the county attorney to determine the best deal you can offer."

"For sure. This is above my pay grade."

"Any chance we can get a yes or no by tomorrow afternoon or evening?"

"I'll make it a priority. But as you know, if someone other than the person who was portrayed to initiate those threats is responsible for them, they were guilty of obstruction of justice."

TWENTY-SEVEN
Getting Some Answers

After completing his supplemental report and getting it off to the Cold Case Unit and the county attorney, a weary but satisfied Pete drove home.

Standing in the nursery and looking down at Teddy, he smiled. He smiled again when he saw Katie sound asleep with an arm across his pillow.

She's guaranteeing she wakes up when I crawl in, he thought.

Katie snuggled up and smiled as he ever so carefully lay his head on the pillow. She kissed his cheek and fell right back to sleep with her head on his chest.

Content and relaxed for the first time in hours, Pete dropped into a deep sleep immediately.

Despite having a short night, Pete woke up at 5:00 as usual. While putting on his running shorts, he heard Teddy stir and loved the change to his plans.

Bending over Teddy's crib, he said, "Good morning, pal. I'm happy to see you. Sorry I missed bedtime last night."

Teddy smiled and reached for him.

Pete lifted him out of his crib and held him tight to his chest. He loved the reassuring feel of Teddy's heartbeat.

"I'm going to have a busy day. How about you, son? Got a mystery to solve, like why Mom doesn't give you more pureed peaches? I love them too." He chuckled.

"How about if we play for a while, until Mom gets up? What do you think, baseball or puzzles?" he asked heading for the hallway.

Intercepting them in the hallway, Katie asked, "What are the two of you conspiring about?"

"Whether to learn to walk or downhill ski first. Care to cast your ballot?" Pete laughed.

"No need. This is not a democracy when it comes to things like that. It's a matriarchy."

"So much for having a voice," Pete said, rubbing Teddy's back.

He put in four miles on the basement treadmill, while Katie nursed Teddy. They multitasked, playing with Teddy while eating breakfast. Reluctantly, Pete left them to shower and shave. At 6:40, he kissed Katie and Teddy goodbye, scratched behind Benji's ears, then rushed out the door.

On the way to headquarters, he thought about how to attack day-three of this investigation. For starters, he and Martin had to go to the airport to review the security footage, trying to determine whether Robert Campbell lied about the time he got there. He had to talk to Commander Lincoln about their discoveries regarding the Golden Rule Building attack ten years ago. He hoped to hear the county attorney's office could help negotiate a deal with Sandra Norcross and her husband. With that, he hoped he and Martin could confirm her ex-husband had nothing to do with the threats sent to David Barrett ... even though that too had nothing to do with their current case. And he hoped to find time to show the photo lineup he created last night to Beth in the coffee shop in the Golden Rule Building.

The minute he reached his office, before he removed his suitcoat or thought about coffee, he called his boss, Senior Commander Lincoln. Protecting his backside, he told him about his unassigned efforts.

If the commander saw or heard about the reports he sent to the Cold Case Unit and the County Attorney last night, he wanted to douse the flames before they exploded into an uncontained wildfire.

Commander Lincoln answered, saying, "Either you solved the Barrett case or it isn't enough to keep you off the streets. Which is it?"

Pete explained about the eyewitness from a decade-old armed assault in the Golden Rule Building—the crime Edgar Waltham was convicted of committing. He and Martin tripped over that eyewitness, while investigating David Barrett's murder. Per that eyewitness's description, Waltham couldn't have done it. Continuing to work the Barrett case, they also learned the threats to Barrett, who was the eyewitness in the Golden Rule case, may have been wrongly attributed to Waltham. "You know me, Commander. I'm doing everything in my power to solve the Barrett murder as quickly as possible. I'd like to continue spending some time on the Waltham case. If my suspicions are correct, I'd like to try to set things in motion to exonerate him. I hope you'll go along with this."

"When you put it that way, how can I reasonably say no. Please keep me posted ... on both cases."

"*Whew*," Pete said after disconnecting, while wiping the sweat off his face.

Next he called the Minneapolis-St. Paul International Airport police office, located in Terminal 1, and spoke with a sergeant. He explained that he and his partner wanted to review the closed-circuit footage from the parking ramps and walkways for 6:00 through 9:30 this past Wednesday morning. "To do that, do we need to do anything besides show up?" he asked.

"Show up and bring lots of refreshments," the Sergeant said. "You could be looking at a four to eight hour, grueling effort."

"Thanks for the tip. I owe you."

"Not a problem. You can pay me back by not requesting my assistance with your efforts." He laughed.

Then Pete looked up the number for Gregory Elko. He still wondered if Elko was the president of the company whose treasurer Barrett suspected of embezzlement.

But Martin interrupted. He walked in, smiling and looking well-rested.

"Spend the night?" he asked.

"Not even close. Don't take off your suit coat. If you need coffee, you can bring it with you. We'll have a busy morning ... watching movies. Or at least CCTV. Excited?"

"I'm trying to catch my breath."

TWENTY-EIGHT
Minneapolis-St. Paul
International Airport (MSP)

Pete and Martin joined the tail end of rush hour traffic. Relying on the emergency lights a few times and Martin's heavy foot the entire way, they reached the Minneapolis-St. Paul International Airport (MSP) at 8:20 a.m.

With a nod from the police officer patrolling the passenger pickup drive-through on the baggage claim level, Martin parked illegally. Then he and Pete hustled to the Airport Police Department's Police Operations Center located by baggage carousel 14.

Pete introduced them and asked for the sergeant he spoke to earlier. That officer set them up in an office with everything they needed to review the security camera footage for the parking ramp and airport ingress and egress walkways.

At 8:35 on this sunny Friday morning, the two investigators pulled their chairs up close and stared at the monitor. They began reviewing the closed circuit TV recordings for Wednesday, September 19, starting at 7:30 a.m. That allowed for their best estimate of how long it would take to get from Barrett's home to the airport, factoring in the time Brian found Dave, and including a large fudge factor.

The good news was, there were multiple cameras in the parking ramp and the walkways, including the stairways, elevators, and skyway between the terminal and the Ground Transportation Center. The bad news was, that multiplied the amount of footage they needed to review.

Looking for Campbell's license plate, they zoomed in on the plate each time the footage picked up a white Honda Pilot. The effort didn't slow them down much. There weren't many white Pilots ... with four wheels, rather than two legs.

After thirty minutes, eyestrain forced them to take a break. So they stood, stretched and rested their eyes.

"Wish I'd thought to bring some eyedrops," Martin said.

By 11:00, they wondered if they'd have to complete the job tomorrow.

"Let's give it another thirty minutes, then make a decision," Pete said.

"You've got my vote," Martin said.

They considered taking turns, but refused after all this time to risk missing anything.

At 11:24, feeling exhausted, both men saw it. A Pilot sped through the ramp far too fast to avoid a crash if someone backed up without paying enough attention.

Do you suppose? they thought, simultaneously.

Pete froze the image and zoomed. He and Martin checked and rechecked the license plate number. They tried to see the driver. They were less successful there. But they got a photo of the Pilot, including the license plate and the time stamp, and the best photo possible of the driver.

The time stamp said 09/19/19 08:32 AM.

"That's two hours later than he told us," Pete said. "If Campbell drove here via David Barrett's home, he'd have been in the height of rush hour. So the trip would take from thirty to forty-five minutes. Add to that the time it took him to get back to his car, wherever he parked it to minimize the chances of it being seen. So, if he's our man, my best guess is that he left David Barrett between 7:30 and 7:55."

"Makes sense to me." Martin nodded.

That detail made the search through the remaining recordings a breeze. But they didn't see Campbell anywhere. Thinking they must have missed him, they went through the footage again, starting five minutes earlier, unlikely as that was, and watched for an additional fifteen minutes, in case he horsed around before leaving his Pilot. The result was the same, but at least they had the photo of his vehicle.

So they packed up, thanked the sergeant, and left, hoping Martin's car remained where he parked it—in a no parking or waiting zone.

The airport police officer who'd ignored Martin's parking violation for more than four hours smiled and nodded as Pete and Martin approached the unmarked car.

There are times when the perks that come with this job can't be beat, Pete thought.

It was 12:30. Anxious to keep things moving, the first thing he'd do was call Robert Campbell's cellphone, hoping. *Do guys like Campbell spend their days in meetings?* he wondered.

He was about to find out.

TWENTY-NINE
A Second Shot at Robert Campbell

"**M**artin," Pete said, "if you think we can get away with it, let's sit here for a few more minutes, while I call Campbell."

"We're about to find out." Martin smiled. "If our friend gets uppity, I'll make the loop out and back a time or two."

Thinking he might get a quicker response to a text than a phone call, Pete sent one, ending with, "Respond ASAP."

As he tucked his phone away, Martin said, "I think we're about to wrap this one up. Don't you agree?"

"I'd like to but, for some reason, I don't have that feeling. And as Grandma Jackie often says, 'Don't count your chickens before they hatch.'"

"But Pete, he lied about the time he reached the airport. Why else would he do that?"

"I hope we're about to find out," Pete said as his phone vibrated.

It was a call from Campbell. "What?" is all he said.

"Where are you?"

"At my office in Golden Valley."

"We need to meet, *now*."

"My day is fully scheduled."

"We'll be there in thirty minutes. It behooves you to see us."

"But ..."

"See you in thirty," Pete interrupted.

Pete took advantage of the trip to Golden Valley to tell Martin what he'd accomplished before going home last night. He also mentioned his conversation with Commander Lincoln this morning.

"So glad you called him," Martin said. "He gives you a lot of leeway, but I was afraid we were getting mighty close to crossing that invisible but critical line."

Pete nodded and said, "I'm hoping to hear from the county attorney's office in the next few hours. If the gods are smiling down on us, maybe we can attempt to back Zach's mom in a corner, after we finish with Campbell."

Martin drove west on I-494 from the airport, then west on I-394 to westbound Olson Memorial Highway, to Douglas Drive North.

As they approached Honeywell's Golden Valley headquarters, Pete's phone vibrated.

"Campbell?" Martin asked.

It wasn't. It was Stephanie from the county attorney's office. "I called the prosecuting attorney," she said. "He said, there's no way to accurately measure the impact of different types of evidence, but the eyewitness identification was definitely the key to the conviction. The threats, especially since they didn't come right out and say the failure to heed the warnings would be fatal, were far less significant. He believes they'd have gotten the conviction without the threats. They wouldn't have gotten it without the eyewitness."

"Did you and the county attorney discuss a possible plea bargain and how far you can go?"

"Yes. It's far more than I anticipated. I think your statement that without a confession you'd never be able to prove their roles clinched it. Do you have a time frame in mind for meeting with them?"

"She works until 3:00 this afternoon. He starts at 7:00 p.m. Martin and I are tied up with our assigned case right now. On our way to a meeting. This could take an hour or more. You're our on-call contact again this evening?"

"Sure am. I'd hate to miss this."

"I'll let you know as soon as I work something out. That should give you at least a half-hour advance notice."

"Talk to you then. I hope this goes according to plan, Pete."

That makes two of us, Pete thought.

Honeywell's Golden Valley campus looked like a sprawling pinwheel with a central building and four large wings. The two-story, brick building had ribbon windows and a glass-roofed, gabled entry atrium at the front of the central building.

Martin parked as close as he could to the atrium in the huge lot that surrounded the building, and Pete notified Campbell of their location.

This was the first time on the Honeywell Campus for both men, and they scanned the area while waiting for Campbell.

He jogged up and stopped alongside Pete's door.

Already knows the pecking order, Martin thought and sighed.

173

They followed Campbell to a large office with windows covering most of one wall and sat across a massive, oak desk from him.

"Okay, let's get this over with," Campbell said.

"You lied to us yesterday," Pete said, not wasting time on niceties.

"What? Prove it!"

"We checked the closed circuit TV surveillance footage from the airport," Pete began. "You arrived two hours later than you said."

Campbell smiled and said, "Explain."

"You pulled into the parking ramp a minute or two before 8:32 on Wednesday. The time you gave us was about 6:30. You also said you left home at 6:00 and went straight to the airport. Why did it take two and a half hours to get there?"

"It didn't. As I said, I arrived about 6:30. I assume your statements are based on the time my Pilot arrived."

Both men nodded.

"Well, you know what they say about assuming anything? I didn't drive the Pilot that morning. A recall was issued in April. It was a timing belt issue that could cause the vehicle to stall. I hadn't taken it in to be inspected. A friend who was flying out later Wednesday morning knew I'd been dragging my feet. He insisted we switch cars on Tuesday evening, and he'd take it in. He's one of those people who hates to let things slide or see his friends do that. He got an appointment, and the dealership promised to get him in and out in plenty of time to catch his flight."

"Friend's name?" Martin asked.

"Bert Forreston."

"Phone number?" Martin asked.

174

After Campbell recited it, Pete said, "Call him now. He's more likely to answer a call from you than from my partner or me. Get him on the phone and hand it to me immediately. Don't tip him off."

Campbell rolled his eyes and did as he was instructed.

Bert told Pete that he and Rob switched cars about 8:00 Tuesday evening, at his prompting. He took Rob's Pilot to Walser Honda on Buck Hill Road in Burnsville on Wednesday morning for a 7:00 appointment. They completed the inspection. He arrived at MSP at about 8:30, parked the car in the long-term ramp, and caught his flight at 9:45. He wore a blue-and-white striped oxford cloth shirt.

"Thanks for your cooperation," Pete told Campbell, and he and Martin returned to the unmarked car.

"Well, that was fun." Martin laughed, just a bit chagrined.

Pete nodded and said, "But I did enjoy the chance to see the Honeywell campus."

Heading back to St. Paul, via eastbound I-394, Pete said, "Lunch or no lunch?"

"Granola bars?" Martin smiled.

Pete had a lot to accomplish to verify Campbell's alibi. First he called Walser Honda in Burnsville to see if there'd been any recalls issued for 2018 Pilots this year. He learned Campbell told the truth. Then he checked whether someone brought in Robert Campbell's 2018 this week. They couldn't say who, but they found an appointment for 7:00 on Wednesday.

THIRTY
Gregory Elko

Opening his notepad, Pete moved on to a lead connected with Barrett's accounting business. He had to determine whether Elko was the person Barrett contacted about the embezzlement. He was about to call, but decided to wait until they reached the other side of the rapidly approaching Lowry Hill tunnel. He wouldn't risk being disconnected almost immediately. Cellphone connections were iffy in the tunnel that stretched a bit more than a quarter mile.

His eyes took a few seconds to adjust to the bright sunlight that assaulted them as they emerged from the tunnel. The mass of lights filling the ceiling of the tunnel didn't prevent that.

Pete smiled when Elko answered. Today was going well, even with Campbell's revelation.

He asked Elko if he spoke with David Barrett on Tuesday.

"Yes, and I saw on the news that someone murdered him the next morning. I can't believe it. It's almost like he was intent on getting some information to me before it was too late. I wish we'd talked longer and that I'd bothered to ask how he was doing. We saw so little of each other the last several years. I guess he was busy with his business, and I with mine. You never know, do you?"

Pete asked, "I understand he spoke with a company president, regarding his suspicions of embezzlement. Was that you?"

"Unfortunately, yes."

"Did you mention David's suspicions to your treasurer?"

"Yes, I accosted him as soon as I got off the phone with Dave."

"How did he react?"

"Exactly as I'd expected. He blew up. He said Dave was a liar and was out to get him. He said Dave felt threatened when Wade criticized his work. I'd suspected the embezzlement, and was anxious to see and hear Dave's evidence. But I didn't wait. That night, I suggested he start looking for another job. You don't suppose ..."

Pete did suppose.

"What's your treasurer's name?" he asked.

"Wade Kellogg."

"How long has he worked for you?"

"Almost ten years. I hired him right out of college. He showed up in my office one day with a gazillion questions and stayed until I had to throw him out, so I could go home."

Pete didn't discourage Gregory's rambling. A critical clue could be wrapped in one of these tidbits. "What does your company do?" he asked.

"Interior decorating. That's why we're located in downtown St. Paul. With all the condos and apartments, we have a built-in clientele. Did you know St. Paul has almost 10,000 residents, and the number of apartments located in downtown has increased by seventy percent since 2010? Lots of those people will make all of their own decorating decisions, but lots won't. Add to that the fact that studies show people in this income group redecorate every three to five years. I'm sitting on a gold mine."

"What's your company's name, and where are you located?" Pete asked.

"Greg Elko Decorating. Original, huh? Wade wanted a hike in pay and to change it to Elko and Kellogg Decorating. Actually, I think he suggested Kellogg and Elko." Greg chuckled. "I gave him a title instead. I didn't take on the title of president until I dubbed him the treasurer. He does the bookkeeping, so I guess it was only fair ... especially since he accepted a title in lieu of more money. We're on the twelfth floor in The Securian Center. I'm sure you already know, but it's on Robert, between 6th and 7th Streets."

"Did Dave tell you how much Kellogg embezzled?"

"No. We were supposed to meet this afternoon. He said he'd pull everything together and build a drum tight case."

"Did you tell Kellogg?"

"No. I just said Dave had all the documentation I needed to prove he was embezzling. You don't think ..." Elko's voice trailed off.

"What do you think?" Pete asked.

I don't believe Wade would do anything like that. I also don't believe in coincidences."

"What kind of car does he drive?" Pete asked.

"It sounds like you suspect him. Do you?"

"We suspect everyone until they clear themselves."

After a pause, Elko said, "A Camaro."

"Year and color?" Pete asked.

2019 and red. I swear he thinks he's eighteen."

"Does he have a family?"

"No kids, and his wife left him five or six years ago. At least that's the way he tells it."

"Do you doubt his veracity?"

"Not as much as I should have, obviously." Elko sighed.

"Where does he live?"

Elko read off the address and said, "That's practically in Dave's back yard."

Pete wrote down the address and asked, "How about his phone numbers, including his work number?"

Pete slowed Elko down as he rattled them off, writing all of them in his notepad.

"Is he at work now?"

"Yes."

"Will he be there in fifteen minutes? We want to drop in and speak with him."

"I'll make sure he is."

"Got a place where my partner and I can meet with him in private?"

"Sure do."

"Are you on a cellphone?"

"Yes, why?"

"As a precaution, I'd like you to head for the elevators and meet us on street level."

"You don't think ..."

"No I don't, but I hate to be wrong. We'll be there almost as fast as you can reach street level. How will I recognize you?"

"I'm wearing navy chinos, a pale-blue button-down shirt, and a light-gray blazer. If that doesn't do it, I'm five feet ten and have blond hair and a blond mustache."

THIRTY-ONE
Wade Kellogg

"Found a replacement for Campbell?" Martin asked as Pete ended his conversation with Elko.

"We're about to find out. Securian Center here we come. Looks like lunch is evading us. Want another granola bar?"

"If you keep this up, we won't get to Sandra Norcross today."

"When did you become such a pessimist, Martin?"

"Actually, when I became a cop and became more aware of all the senseless deaths," Martin said pensively.

Taking the 6th Street exit off I-94, Martin found a parking space within a reasonable distance of Elko's offices. After so much sitting, he and Pete both appreciated a chance to stretch their legs.

Walking into the center, Pete and Martin spied the blond man standing near the elevators instantly, despite the abundance of Scandinavians living in Minnesota.

Pete nodded when Greg looked at him questioningly, and Greg hurried over to him and Martin.

Elko said, "I've been watching the elevators, in case Wade suspected something and decided to bolt. He doesn't have any meetings scheduled for the rest of the day, so he won't have an excuse not to meet with you."

The three men rode the elevators to the twelfth floor, then went right to Elko's kingdom.

Entering Greg Elko Decorating, Pete thought, *This is a great calling card. I'd love to have him advise Katie and me if we ever get around to finding a new home.*

The client waiting area contained two warm-brown leather chairs. A round table between them held a woven basket filled with fresh fruits. Neat stacks of architectural and designer magazines covered a low-profile walnut coffee table. The plush cream-colored wool rug and a floor lamp cast a warm glow over the area.

Martin saw the fruit and thought about taking a detour to grab an apple. He resisted.

The teal-colored carpet in Elko's office enhanced the three dove-gray and one charcoal-colored walls. His desk was a contemporary, sleek, walnut. It held a huge monitor and carefully arranged swatches of a variety of color schemes. To the left was a sitting area with three curve-back armchairs and a round table displaying decorating magazines.

Passing his office, Elko led Pete and Martin back to Wade Kellogg's office, and introduced them to Kellogg.

Kellogg popped up out of his chair as they entered and eyed the two investigators. They saw a trim six footer. He had medium-brown hair, deep-set brown eyes, and a square jaw. He wore navy chinos, a bright-blue shirt, and a gray herringbone blazer.

His wooden desk had metal legs and a high-backed leather chair. Two emerald-green, velvet chairs faced the desk. Everything sat on a geometric patterned rug.

Pete and Martin introduced themselves, and Kellogg shook their hands with a bone-cracking grip. Pete wondered if he wanted to prove something ... or send a message.

"We have some questions," Pete said.

Kellogg shrugged, pointed at the velvet chairs, and sat back down behind his desk.

"No, we'd prefer you come to our office," Pete said. "We have a nice, comfortable place to sit and well-stocked vending machines. My partner and I haven't had lunch. We'll get something to eat there."

Kellogg offered them an apple or a peach.

"Thanks, but I want something more substantial," Pete said. "How about you, Martin?"

"For sure."

"Are you buying?" Kellogg asked.

"You bet," Pete said.

He nodded at Elko as they passed him on the way to the elevator.

Pete and Martin bought their lunch from the vending machines and bought mixed nuts, a granola bar, and lemon-flavored sparkling water for Kellogg. Then Martin got him settled in an interview room. Meanwhile, Pete set up the video and audio recording equipment.

Pete began the interview by asking, "How did you get into interior decorating, Mr. Kellogg?"

"I prefer Wade, and I loved watching what my mom accomplished with a very limited budget. She made my day each time she permitted me to help in any way at all."

"How long have you been doing it?" Pete asked.

"Almost since the day I graduated from college."

"How long ago was that?" Pete asked.

"It was ten years last May."

"Does it require specific coursework?" Pete asked.

"I have a bachelor's from the U in marketing and took numerous art classes, as well as several in accounting. I also have an interior decorating certificate from Metro State University."

"How did you link up with Greg?" Pete asked.

"He decorated a condo in Galtier owned by one of my mom's friends. Mom took me to see it, and the friend showed me the decorator's business card. I was a junior in college and thought being an interior decorator with an office in downtown was the epitome. A year later, I went to Greg's office to put out feelers, doing my best to sell him on the value of having me as an assistant. It was harder than I'd anticipated, but eventually I succeeded." Wade smiled.

"How long have you kept the books for Greg?" Martin asked.

Frowning, Wade repositioned himself on the chair and said, "Almost as long as I've worked for him. He likes fabrics much more than numbers. I offered to take the bookkeeping off his hands. I wanted to repay him for giving me a job."

"I understand David Barrett recently challenged the accuracy of some of your bookkeeping," Martin said.

Wade was up like a shot and sneered, "So I was told, by Gregg, *not* Dave. How dare Dave not bring it to my attention first? How would you feel if someone second guessed you and didn't have the decency to discuss it with you before going to your boss?"

"I'd be angry," Martin said.

"I'm glad you understand." Kellogg nodded.

"Where were you Wednesday morning between 6:00 and 9:30?" Martin asked.

"I was home until 7:00. Then I went for a run. That took forty-five or fifty minutes. I got back home around 7:45 or 7:50, showered and got ready for work. I was out the door and on my way downtown at about 8:15. I arrived here about 8:35 or 8:40. If you're looking for someone to verify that, I have a security system at home that logs my comings and goings, and Greg arrived here just before 9:00 and knows I was here until 9:30. The rest of the time is a matter of either you believe me or you don't."

"I'm a runner," Pete said. "My mornings are never complete if I don't run before work. Where did you run?"

"Around Lake Phalen."

"It's a great run, isn't it?" Pete said. "I have a six-month-old son, so these days too many of my runs are on a treadmill. It isn't the same, is it."

"It's not even close. I'd rather run through a half foot of fresh snow."

"Have you ever been to David Barrett's home?" Pete asked.

"Why would I go there?"

"I thought you might stop by to drop off or pick up documents, records, files, whatever," Pete said.

"No, I've never been there."

"But you know where he lived, don't you," Pete said.

"So what? Is that against the law?"

"No law I'm aware of," Pete said.

"Was David right? Were you embezzling funds from Greg's company?" Martin asked.

Wade's face reddened as he slammed a hand down on the table and yelled, "Of course not! I owe where I am today to Gregg."

"You kept the books," Martin said, "so you knew how much money came in and went out. Did he treat you fairly when it came to your paycheck?"

Kellogg's head dropped. He rubbed his neck and said, "I asked for a raise. He gave me a title. That sufficed initially. I knew he could afford to pay me more. I do excellent work, and I've helped him grow his business."

"Did you tell him that?" Martin asked.

Wade nodded.

"And?" Martin asked.

"He said 'In good time.'"

"When was that?" Pete asked.

"Last Christmas."

"That seemed like too much time?" Pete asked.

"For sure!"

"And?" Pete asked.

Wade shrugged.

"Did Greg talk to you about David Barrett's suspicions?" Pete asked.

"Talk? I wouldn't call it talking. He all but screamed as he accused me of stealing from him. He said he was meeting with David on Friday, and David would provide the proof."

"Did you try to defend yourself?" Pete asked.

"Without having the books in front of me, how could I? Even with them, I doubt he'd have taken my word over David's. I knew once David met with Greg, I'd be history. Interior decorators have their associations, and they're a tight knit group. I'll bet every one of them in the seven county Metro area has already heard about David's accusations. I'll never get another job in this field. Interior decorating is my life. I may have made an error or two, but I *never* embezzled a dime! And I don't have enough money to open my own business. Even if I did, thanks to the power of word of mouth, customers would run from an interior decorator who's believed to be an embezzler." Wade covered his face with his hands.

"Where do you live?" Martin asked.

"On Kennard."

"That's not far from David Barrett's home, is it?" Martin asked.

"No."

"But you've never been to his home?" Martin asked.

Wade stared at his clasped hands and said, "No, never."

"You began working with Greg ten years ago," Pete said. "Are you aware that was also when David testified against an armed robber, despite the threats resulting from his agreeing to do so?"

Wade stared at Pete and shook his head.

Pete Mirandized Kellogg, explaining it was mandatory, then said, "As you can well imagine, David did everything he could think of to protect himself and his wife. Did it ever occur to you that he might have installed a video doorbell when they were still cutting edge?" He hoped Kellogg would buy the doorbell David and Melissa never did.

Wade's face went white.

"You're a young man, Wade. You have a lot of years ahead of you. This was premeditated, so you're looking at first degree murder. That means life in prison with no possibility of parole. Based on what I've seen and what you've said this afternoon, I don't think you're evil. If you're willing to confess, I'll call the county attorney's office. You might be able to work out a plea bargain. Do you want to try?"

Wade swallowed hard and stared silently at the table.

Neither Pete nor Martin rushed him. After a protracted pause, Wade said, "If I plea bargain, what kind of deal might I get?"

"Only the county attorney can make that offer," Pete said. "I can call an assistant county attorney and request they discuss it with the county attorney. This will take some time. Want me to do that?"

A defeated-looking Kellogg closed his eyes and nodded.

Martin got Kellogg another beverage and some snacks, while Pete went to his office and called their representative in the county attorney's office.

He explained to Pamela, the assistant county attorney, that he and Martin were investigating a case. They had a suspect who had the means, motive, and opportunity. They were sure he was guilty of first degree murder, but the case was weak. A search warrant might solve that, but they didn't have the evidence to get one. He explained the suspect had no prior convictions, and it appeared he'd confess if offered a plea bargain.

"I know you have to go to the top with this," he said. "Can you speak with the county attorney this afternoon and determine what you can offer? I know I'm sounding like a broken record, because I made this request yesterday for another case, but these are important confessions, and I believe justice will be served. If you and the county attorney come up with an offer, I'd like you to come to headquarters to offer the plea bargain, and witness the confession."

"You know what, Pete? At this rate, we'll have to hire another assistant county attorney just for you. I can't make any promises. Let me see what I can do. I know you needed the answer yesterday, so I'll do my best to move things along. I'll get back to you as fast as I can."

Pete thanked Pamela, then called the coffee shop in the Golden Rule Building to see if Beth was still there.

"For a few more minutes," a woman said.

Pete asked to speak with her and was put on hold for several minutes, wondering if Beth left while he was on hold. He recognized her voice immediately as she said, "Are you looking for Beth, sweetie?"

Pete identified himself, said he understood she was leaving shortly, and asked when he could meet with her.

"I can't hang around this afternoon, dear, and I don't work tomorrow. But give me a time when you can be here tomorrow, and I'll stop in. I'll be downtown anyway."

Not knowing tomorrow's schedule, it was hard to commit to a time. So Pete grabbed a time out of the air and said 10:00, if that worked for her.

It did, and he decided he and Martin would work around it.

Then he checked his email to burn a little time before he returned to Martin and Kellogg.

"The county attorney is working on it," he said when he joined them. "It's Friday afternoon. That could work for or against us when it comes to how long it will take. Anyone need a bathroom break?"

"I wondered how much longer I'd have to wait," Kellogg said.

Martin accompanied him, and Pete bought a Diet Coke. Back in the interview room, he was opening it when his phone vibrated. He glanced at the screen and saw it was the county attorney's office.

"On the way to my car," Pamela said. "Can't decide if you're lucky or have some special connection. The county attorney was walking out of his office, car keys in hand, when I reached him. I said I had to speak with him today, not Monday. Figured if it cost me my job, you'd help me find another." She chuckled.

"We discussed the case. I told him you said it was weak, but you are sure that the suspect did it. Explained you believe a plea bargain is the only way to get a conviction. We debated back and forth. He agreed to second degree murder. Want me to make that offer?"

"Fantastic. Please."

"See you shortly."

Pete told Martin and Kellogg the assistant county attorney was on her way, then returned to his office.

Pamela arrived ten minutes later. She looked harried. "I wonder if someone can show me how to block your calls on Friday afternoons." She smiled.

Anxious to get things moving, they hurried to the interview room where Martin and Kellogg waited for them.

Pete brought another chair for Pamela and set it on his and Martin's side of the table. Then he introduced Pamela to Wade Kellogg.

Pamela dove right in. "I spoke with the county attorney," she said. "It took a lot of fast talking, but I convinced him to offer you a plea bargain of second degree murder. First degree means life in prison with no parole. Second degree means up to forty years, but you have no prior convictions, correct?"

Kellogg nodded.

"In that case, you're generally talking twelve-and-a-half to fifteen years. In Minnesota, you serve the first two-thirds of that time in prison and the last third on supervised release. Are you interested?"

Wade sighed and said, "I guess it's the best I can hope for, isn't it?"

"Yes," Pamela said, "and it's worlds better than the alternative. However, it's contingent on your confession fulfilling the investigators' requirements."

"Understood, and I know I have the right to an attorney. But I don't want anyone thinking they know what's best for me and telling me what to do. So I'll plead guilty to second degree murder."

"Start at the beginning, Wade," Pete said. "You said earlier that you left home at 7:00 and went for a run. Do you want to change that?"

"No. It was true then, and it's true now."

"Where did you go on that run?" Pete asked.

"I ran from home to Lake Phalen. Then I ran around the lake until I was across the street from David Barrett's home. I'd done some scouting and as best I could tell, he left for work between 7:25 and 7:30. I crossed the street and ran up to his house at 7:15. I couldn't risk missing him."

"And?" Pete asked.

"He has pavers around his shrubs. I brought a screw driver to dislodge one. With the screwdriver, it took just seconds. I took the paver and hid behind a huge bush just right of his garage door. I hid there until I heard the garage door begin opening." Wade sighed and took a few deep breaths.

"Then?" Martin asked.

"I heard him walk out of the house and toward his car. I peered around the wall. I needed to know where he was. I wanted to reach him before he got in his car. I didn't want to see his face. I couldn't hit him over the head with him looking at me. He'd just reached the tail end of the car. He still had to go around it to the driver's side. I waited about two seconds and looked again. He was turning the corner and about to walk along the driver's side. I walked as fast and as quietly as I could, thankful for my Nikes."

Wade closed his eyes and ran his fingers through his hair. Sweat moistened his forehead. After several seconds, he continued. "I stood behind him, lifted the paver, and hit him twice on the crown. The end of the paver broke off. I was mesmerized, watching a chunk of it fly back at me. I was afraid it would hit me in the face. I was so worried about that, I didn't see David go down. I snapped back when I heard his body hit the cement. I almost screamed. Then I turned and ran back to the lake and home as fast as I could. By the time I got home, my heart beat so hard and so fast, I thought I was having a heart attack. I stood in the shower a long time, trying to relax and calm down."

"Describe the location, relative to the car, where David's body came to rest and the position," Martin said.

"He lay face down on the driver's side. His feet were by the rear, driver's side wheel."

"How did you know he was dead?" Martin asked.

"I didn't. By then, I didn't want him to be."

"Why did you use a paver?" Martin asked.

"I saw them when I scouted his home, determining what time he left in the morning. I don't own a gun, and I knew I couldn't stab him. It was convenient."

"You had to dig it up. Your hands must have been coated with dirt," Martin said.

Wade shook his head and said, "I brought a pair of gardening gloves."

"Where are they now?" Martin asked.

"I turned them inside out and dumped them in a trash can I passed downtown on my way to work that morning."

"You bought the gloves once you decided to do this?" Martin asked.

Wade shook his head. "I bought them to plant the shrubs in my front yard."

"What kind of car did David drive?" Martin asked, continuing to verify they had the right guy.

"A royal blue BMW."

"Describe the location of the paver you pried up," Pete said.

"If you're looking at the house from the street, it was along the right side of the large bush I mentioned and partially hidden by the bush."

"What color are his pavers?" Pete asked.

"Dark gray."

"How large a piece broke off the paver?" Pete asked.

Wade used his thumb and forefinger to indicate it was about one inch.

"Is that the length or the width?" Pete asked.

"The chunk was the width of the paver, so I guess that was the length."

"You said you watched it break off and fall. Where did it lie with respect to the car?" Pete asked.

"It bounced off my jacket and dropped. I only know it ended up by David's lower legs or ankles."

"What happened to the rest of the paver?" Pete asked.

"When I left him lying there, I ran down the driveway, across the street, and to the path along the lake. After several steps, and after I'd checked to make sure no one was watching, I tossed it as far as I could, out into the lake."

"Whereabouts was that?" Pete asked.

"I don't know. By then, I was so rattled, I was just acting, not thinking."

"What kind of jacket were you wearing?" Pete asked.

"A polyester or nylon windbreaker. I'm not sure what it's made of."

"What happened to the screwdriver?" Pete asked.

"I know I overreacted, but I threw it away with the gloves."

Pete told Wade they'd be back in a few minutes, and he, Martin, and Pamela walked out the door and huddled too far away for Wade to hear them.

"What do you think, Martin?" Pete asked.

"He convinced me. He knows all the details, including those not released to the media, like the murder weapon, that the end broke off, and where it landed."

Pete said, "Forensics didn't find any fibers on the piece of the paver that broke off and that he said bounced off his jacket. With a nylon or polyester windbreaker, that's reasonable. Are you satisfied?" he asked Pamela.

"As long as you're convinced it's a valid confession, yes. It should be all we need to present the case and the plea bargain to the judge. I can't see a judge nixing the plea bargain.

"Thanks for all your help," Pete said. "Needless to say, we couldn't have done it without you."

"Glad it worked as well as it did," Pamela said.

"You know the other plea bargain I mentioned?" Pete asked. "I worked that one out with Stephanie. Our next mission is to move that case along far enough to contact her."

"Should I say a prayer for her?" Pamela smiled.

"Couldn't hurt." Pete nodded.

He re-entered the interview room and escorted Wade to the Ramsey County jail. On the way, he said, "I'm sorry it's Friday afternoon. That means you won't see the judge until Monday morning. I appreciate your cooperation and will pray for you."

"Thanks. It's going to be a long nine or ten years. How could I be so stupid?"

When Pete reached his office, Martin was there waiting for him. He wondered if Pete could handle another few hours like the last few.

Pete answered that question when he said, "Let's go, Martin. Too late to talk to Beth, but Zach's mom, Sandra, got off an hour ago and Thad doesn't go to work for several hours."

THIRTY-TWO

Sandra Norcross

Martin took I-35E south, exited at East 7th Street and headed east until they reached Phalen Boulevard. He then went north to the neighborhood where Zach lived with his mother and stepfather. They lived almost as close to Lake Phalen as David Barrett, but in a home several rungs down the economic ladder.

Their Payne-Phalen neighborhood of Northeast St. Paul was developed during the post-WWI housing boom. An end to the labor and materials shortages that went hand-in-hand with the war fueled the boom. A rapid population growth due to the migration of rural Minnesotans and immigrants seeking industrial jobs in Minneapolis and St. Paul also played a major role. Their neighborhood consisted of homes similar to their two-story craftsman and built between 1918 and 1924 on compact lots.

This time, Martin pounded on the door and yelled, "Police! Open the door!"

Hearing the commotion coming from the other side of the door, Pete wondered if they'd just unleashed a demon. He and Martin unbuttoned their suitcoats, making their Glocks readily accessible.

A woman's voice called out, "Why are you here? What do you want? You must have the wrong house!"

"We're here to speak with Zachary Waltham," Martin yelled. "Let us in, *now*!"

"He isn't home," a shaky version of the female voice said.

"According to our records," Pete called back, "that's his red Honda Civic. Don't make things worse than they already are. The best thing you can do for yourself and Zachary is to cooperate."

After a protracted pause, she said, "Okay."

A minute later, Pete and Martin heard the unmistakable clunk of a deadbolt. A woman who matched the driver's license photo of Sandra Norcross opened the door.

She was fifty-two, five feet six, and 130 pounds. Her gray-streaked brown hair was pulled back in a tight bun, her brown eyes peered through glasses with thin brown frames, and red lipstick made the most of her small mouth. She still wore her uniform—scrubs.

An astonished Zach stood twenty paces behind her at the foot of the original oak stairway.

Pete walked past Sandra and up to Zach, holding his handcuffs. "We have to question you at headquarters," he said. "Coming willingly or do I need to arrest you?"

"I don't get it!" Zach said, looking questioningly at Pete. "What now?"

"We know you were part of the group that prepared and delivered threats to a David Barrett in an effort to keep him from testifying against your dad some ten years ago. We now have proof that your dad didn't prepare or deliver the notes or phone calls. We know you know who did. If you cooperate, we'll go easy on you. If you refuse ..." Pete frowned and shook his head.

"He's a minor!" Sandra shouted. "You can't question him unless a parent is present."

"His father will be there," Pete said.

"No! I'll go. You have to let me."

"It's not going to be a picnic," Pete said. "I think you should let his father handle this."

"Are you suggesting a woman can't handle it?" Sandra snarled.

"No, I'm saying if I were you, I'd avoid it, not run in blindly."

Sandra opened the entryway closet door. She grabbed a jacket and her purse. "Okay, let's go," she said.

"We're required to take Zachary in our car," Pete said. "Do you know where headquarters is on Grove Street?"

"No. What's the address?"

Pete waited for her to get a pen and paper, then recited it.

"We'll wait until you arrive before starting, unless you aren't there in twenty minutes," Pete said. "It shouldn't take you nearly that long. Just park in the lot, walk in the main door, and ask for me." He handed her his business card. Then he and Martin led Zach out the front door and to the unmarked car.

Zach didn't say a word until Martin started the car and pulled out into traffic. Then he said, "Wow, if I didn't know better, I'd think you were serious."

"We are," Pete said. "The rules changed between the time we left your dad's and arrived here."

"I don't get it," Zach said. "I told you Mom and Thad did it, and you're going to arrest me?"

He thought for a few miles, then said, "You're testing her, seeing if she'll speak up to keep me from being arrested."

Pete didn't respond.

When they reached HQ, Martin set Zach up in an interview room.

Meanwhile, Pete called Stephanie, the on-call assistant county attorney with whom he'd made arrangements. "We're at headquarters and waiting for his mother to arrive," he said. "I'm giving you a heads up, like I promised. We're hoping to need your assistance in a half hour or so. If we fail, I'll let you know that too."

He'd barely disconnected when Sandra came rushing in, out of breath.

Martin got her settled next to Zach, and Pete began, announcing the date, time, and the names of the people present.

"Zachary Waltham," he said, sounding even more officious than normal, "we have you here today to discuss your involvement in the preparation and delivery of the instruments that played a significant role in the conviction of Edgar Waltham in 2009. The murder of David Barrett, the recipient of the aforementioned instruments exacerbates the problem. In addition, your known presence in the vicinity of that murder on the date and time it was committed also indicates your likely participation. We will do our best to have you tried as an adult, seeking a sentence of life in prison. We have proof of your participation in the creation of the threats against Barrett." Then he Mirandized Zach before saying, "Is there anything you'd like to say in your defense?"

A wide-eyed Zach shook his head.

"You can't do this!" Sandra screamed. "I don't know what you think you have that proves Zach was involved in the preparation and delivery of the threats, but I know for certain he wasn't!"

"And how can you possibly know that, Mrs. Norcross?" Pete asked. "It's difficult to prove a negative.

In other words, that someone didn't do something. It's far easier to prove they did. That gives my partner and me the advantage here." Pete smiled.

Sandra and Zachary sat wordlessly, side by side, staring at the table separating them from Pete and Martin.

Pete gave them a couple of minutes, then said, "Okay, Zachary. Let's go to the jail. I'll get you booked. You'll be arraigned on Monday."

Sandra jumped up, knocking her chair over, and exclaimed, "No, stop!"

"I'm sorry, ma'am," Pete said. "I hate to see a young life destroyed this way, but there's nothing we can do for him." He motioned to Zach to come to his side of the table.

"But he was seven when those things happened. You can't possibly think a seven-year-old should be sent to prison."

"We're aware, based on his performance in grade school, high school, and college, that Zachary operated far above the level of most kids his age. In this case, that's unfortunate. The best you can hope for is that the judge will consider his age when it comes to the sentencing. Come on son, let's go." Pete turned and reached for the door.

"What if I prove he had nothing to do with it?" Sandra asked.

"That's probably the only thing that will save him." Pete said.

"Can we work a deal? On TV, people are always working deals."

"The county attorney has to do that. Do you want me to ask them to send someone over?"

Sandra wiped away a tear and nodded.

"Okay, but it could be awhile. I hope you're not wasting our time. It's been a long week for my partner and me. You won't get any points for jerking our chains. If we drag the county attorney over here for nothing, you won't make any points there either."

"*Please*, I have to talk to someone who can work a deal in exchange for the information I can provide."

Looking at Zach and pointing to Sandra's side of the table, Pete said, "Sit back down, Zachary. I'll be back as soon as possible."

Martin stayed in the interview room, while Pete returned to his office and called Stephanie.

Thanks to the heads up he'd provided, she was ready to go when he called. She arrived at headquarters within ten minutes.

During that time, Martin kept things calm in the interview room by providing pop and snacks.

Two faces tensed up and one relaxed when Pete and Stephanie entered the interview room.

Pete introduced Stephanie to Sandra and Zach.

Stephanie said, "I understand you have some information you believe valuable to us. However, you're concerned about sharing it without some special consideration. Is that correct?"

Sandra nodded, wringing her hands.

"Does anyone else know about this? If so, they too must share their information."

Sandra's jaw dropped. After a long pause, she said, "There is one other person."

"The special consideration you're requesting will be contingent on that person also providing a statement. Will they?"

Sandra nodded and said, "First, tell me about the special consideration you'll grant."

"What kind of consideration are you seeking?"

"I insist on a full pardon in exchange for revealing who is responsible for the preparation and delivery of those threats. That includes there being no record of this. Having a record could keep me from continuing in my current job."

Stephanie looked at Pete and Martin and said, "We need to confer. Let's step out in the hallway."

After moving away from the interview room, she asked for their opinions.

"In light of what you told me this morning," Pete said, I'm in favor of agreeing not to charge her with the crime. But I think she needs to understand you can't release her from the civil case the person convicted, her ex-husband, may file."

Martin nodded.

"Can you do what she asks?" Pete asked. "Or do you first need to meet again with the county attorney?"

"I'm glad you gave me a heads up. Yes, I can and I'm willing to do it, if they agree to community service. What do you think?"

"Specifically?" Pete asked.

"Since they both work full time and after what I learned from the prosecuting attorney regarding the minor, if any part those threats played in the conviction, I think 250 hours for her. If her husband was less involved, perhaps 150 for him, depending on what he tells us. Too stiff?"

Pete and Martin thought it was generous.

The three of them reentered the interview room, and Stephanie made the offer. She explained it was contingent on anyone else with information about the threats coming in and answering their questions. She said the judge would make the final decision about the number of hours of community service. Then she explained this dealt only with the criminal charges that could be filed against her. "The person to whom the threats were attributed can still file civil charges," she said.

Sandra looked taken aback at that last point. But she sighed, thought a moment, and asked, "Will you grant the other person the same special considerations?"

"Yes, unless their part in it was more egregious."

"Can I make a phone call?" Sandra asked.

"Go ahead, if you're contacting others connected with the threats," Stephanie said.

Sandra lifted her purse onto her lap and rustled around inside, until she found her phone. "Can I have a minute of privacy?" she asked.

"We'll be right outside," Pete said. "Let us know when you're ready to continue. Come with us, Zachary," he added.

Pete told Zach there was no longer any need for him to be there and gave him cab fare to get home.

"But I want to stay." Zach groaned.

"According to the Rolling Stones," Pete said, "'*You Can't Always Get What You Want.*' Your mom is sticking her neck out for you. If you were her, would you want your son to hear what she's about to say?"

"No," he sighed and turned to walk away.

"And Zach," Pete said.

Zach looked back over his shoulder, and Pete said, "Good luck."

"For a minute," Stephanie said, "I thought you were going to break into song."

"I would have, but the fact I could have made it in a rock band is a closely kept secret."

"Then why didn't you?" she asked.

"Their hours are even worse than ours."

Moments later, Sandra opened the door and looked out. "Thad is on his way, reluctantly."

"Then let's get this over with," Pete said and Mirandized her.

Sandra admitted she dreamt up the telephone and mailed threats. She recruited her husband's assistance in creating and delivering them. "Zachary," she said, "had absolutely no part in it."

To insure she was telling the truth, Pete asked, "How did you prevent DNA and fingerprints from being found on the letters?"

"Neither Thad nor I, his real name is Thaddeus, touched the paper or envelopes. We used surgical gloves, and we used a sponge to moisten the envelope flap," she said, repeating what Zach had remembered.

"How did you keep the phone calls from being traced back to you?" Pete asked.

"I made Thad use a pay phone."

"Which pay phone or pay phones?" Pete asked, knowing it was hard to find one anymore.

"There's one outside the SuperAmerica on Rice and Wheelock Parkway. It's mounted on a post just south of the building. I told Thad to use that one. That way, he didn't have to go inside, where the employees might remember him. And he wouldn't have to get out of his car and try to keep his back turned to anyone driving in or at the pumps."

"Who came up with the wording for the written threats?" Martin asked.

"Me," she said, tapping her chest with an index finger.

"How about the verbal ones?" Martin asked.

"I wrote and rewrote the wording for both about a dozen times. I made Thad memorize the phone call one and repeat it to me until he did it perfectly."

"Why should we believe Zachary was in no way involved?" Martin asked.

"Talk to him. He loves his dad. He'd never do anything to hurt him, and we did all this while he was in school."

Pete looked at Martin and Stephanie, and both nodded, so he said, "That's all we need from you, Sandra. As long as Thaddeus' story matches yours, we're finished with you."

"Can I sit in the room while you speak with him? He might feel a lot better and be better able to answer your questions with me there."

"Sorry, no," Pete said. "But I'll find a place for you to wait for him."

Sandra wasn't happy but accepted it.

THIRTY-THREE
Thaddeus Norcross

By the time Martin had Sandra settled in a waiting area, Thad was there, shifting nervously from foot-to-foot.

Pete got him situated in an interview room, waited for Stephanie and Martin to join them, then Mirandized him. That freaked out Thaddeus until Pete explained this was exactly what they did with Sandra. He told Thad everything he said was being recorded with both audio and video.

"Why do you have to do that?"

"Did Sandra explain the breaks we're giving you for doing this?" Pete asked.

Thad nodded.

"If you lie to us," Pete said, "they're canceled."

"Does Sandy know that?"

"Yes," Pete said. "Telling the truth is always a condition for a plea bargain."

"Makes sense."

"First," Pete said, "what was the purpose for the threats?"

"I don't think I should say."

"Are you aware Sandra's plea bargain depends on you answering our questions?" Pete asked. "It does."

"Sandy wanted to hurt Edgar. She thought this would do that. She said it made him look even more guilty of the crime they'd arrested him for."

"Who wrote the messages you mailed to the guy they were supposed to frighten?" Pete asked.

"Sandy. She's better than me at stuff like that."

"How about the phone calls? Who decided what to say?"

"Sandy. She knew better than me how to make them convincing."

"Who made the phone calls?" Martin asked.

"Me." Thaddeus shrank in his chair.

"Did you use your home phone?" Martin asked.

Thaddeus shook his head and said, "Didn't want them traced back to us."

"So, what did you do?" Pete asked.

"Used a pay phone."

"One pay phone or did you use a different one for each call?"

Thaddeus held up an index finger.

"Which pay phone?" Pete asked.

"Do you know the SuperAmerica on Rice and Wheelock?"

Pete nodded.

"That one, and only that one."

"Who put the messages in the envelopes and licked the flap to seal them?" Pete asked.

"Sandy put them in the envelopes, but don't look for her fingerprints. She wore surgical gloves. We used a damp sponge instead of licking the flaps to seal them."

"Anything else we need to know?" Pete asked.

"Sandy isn't a bad person. Edgar hurt her. That's why she did it."

When Stephanie told Thaddeus he was required to do 150 hours of community service, he smiled and said, "Sandy said she got 250. Thanks for giving me a break."

Martin took Thad to Sandy, and Thad's face lit up when he saw her.

She smiled at him and asked Martin, "Are we set?"

"Yes, and you're free to go. Thanks for your cooperation."

"They gave me 150 hours, Thad told Sandra. I'll be cursing Zach for the first 149."

"What about the last hour?" she asked.

"I'll be celebrating the fact I'm almost done."

Curious, Martin thought. *She's the one who got him involved in the scheme. It wouldn't have happened without her. Yet he blames the kid whose only role was as the bargaining chip. Second thought, without Zach, we wouldn't have known they masterminded the threats.*

Martin returned to Pete and Stephanie in time to hear Pete ask her to forward him a copy of the report she prepared for the county attorney. He wanted it for his meeting with Commander Lincoln ... and possibly others, depending on what happened next with Edgar Waltham.

"We're meeting with Beth at 10:00 tomorrow morning," he told Martin as Stephanie packed up her things to return to the county attorney's offices downtown.

"Tell me it doesn't involve a plea bargain." She laughed.

"It doesn't involve a plea bargain," Pete said.

"For real or are you just doing as I asked?"

"For real. But it's part of the same case we're not working, as are the confessions you just helped us obtain."

"How does Commander Lincoln feel about all of this?" she asked.

"Well, as of 5:50 this beautiful Friday afternoon, I'm still employed." He smiled.

"Notice he said 'I' not 'we,' Stephanie," Martin said. "Should I be drawing any conclusions from that?" He didn't feel as paranoid as he sounded.

The afternoon took a lot out of both investigators, even though they hadn't confessed to anything. That gave them a feel for what the person under the microscope felt like.

"Let's call it a day, Martin. That way, we can spend some time with our families. We'll meet here at 9:30 tomorrow morning, so we get to Beth's coffee shop early."

"What if Beth doesn't pick out the one with the record, the one you're thinking committed the armed assault Waltham was convicted of? Will you give up or search for another way?"

"Yes."

THIRTY-FOUR
Ending Day Two and Beginning Day Three

Pete called and told Katie he'd arrive home about 6:20. She delayed dinner, looking forward to spending time with him and hearing about the case they must have solved. He wouldn't come home this early otherwise. *Not even Teddy could induce that*, she thought and smiled.

"Guess who's going to rock and sing you to sleep tonight," she told Teddy, who sat in his highchair, watching her prepare dinner. He played with his teething ring, a rattle, and his favorite stuffed animal, a puppy, while he watched her and listened to her monologue.

Benji had finished his dinner. He lay on the floor beside the highchair, head on his paws, watching Katie and Teddy. He hoped one of them would drop some tidbits on the floor. Cleanup was his favorite job.

Hearing the garage door, Katie lifted Teddy out of his highchair and sped to the back door. She was anxious to greet Pete as he walked in. She loved the look on his face each time they did this. It said, "I love my life with you guys!"

Opening the door, the first thing she saw was how exhausted he looked. But when he saw them, his face lit up. He stepped inside and gave Katie and Teddy a group hug. Then he kissed Katie and Teddy, and he rubbed Benji's ears.

"Does it get better than this?" he asked.

"Not in my book," Katie said, handing Teddy to Pete.

"Have you missed me?" Pete asked, lifting a squealing Teddy up over his head.

"He has. This afternoon, he asked how many hours until you retire."

"And what did you tell him?"

"That he won't be able to count that high for another six months or so." Katie smiled.

"What did he say to that?"

"As long as you're happy. That's the important thing."

"It's also important the two of you are happy. Are you?"

"Happier than I could ever have imagined before I met you, Pete."

That bought her a much better kiss than the one she got when he arrived.

They sat Teddy in his activity center and watched him swat at and spin the multicolored shapes. He especially loved anything that made a sound.

A few minutes before 7:00, when Teddy was ready for bed, Pete scooped him up in his arms, walked to the nursery, and got comfortable in the rocking chair. He rocked and sang "*Hush little baby, don't say a word ...*" until Teddy was sound asleep. Then he placed him gently in his crib, even though it was unlikely the movement would wake Teddy up.

Benji took that as his signal to park himself in front of the crib, doing guard duty.

When Pete returned to the kitchen, Katie had their dinner in her hands and was on her way to the dining room. So he got the tea pot and two mugs.

Over dinner, Pete told Katie about his and Martin's progress with both cases, including how committed he was to investigating whether the person convicted a decade ago was actually guilty.

"And if he isn't?" she asked.

"I'll work on getting him exonerated," Pete sighed.

"It's no wonder I love you," Katie said and kissed him again.

That night, they eventually fell asleep, still wrapped in each other's arms.

Saturday morning, dawn broke as Pete drove to HQ. His timing would have forced him to miss the sunrise, but this morning, the clouds did that anyway. It was 63° when he left home, and the predicted high was 77°.

Glorious for mid-September, he thought.

He reached headquarters at his usual: 7:00. He'd have liked to spend more time with Teddy and Katie, but decided to save that for later in the day. He was anxious to get started on the paperwork required to close out David Barrett's murder case. A plethora of forms had to be completed to accomplish that.

Another priority was, he hoped, helping to provide the information required to overturn Edgar Waltham's conviction, assuming he was right. If Beth identified Todd Trimont as the person she saw in the Golden Rule Building ten years ago, he hoped that would be enough to get things moving.

How much can and will Commander Lincoln do? he wondered. He hoped to know that a short time after he and Martin met with Beth. He set an 8:00 alarm on his cellphone. That's when he'd text the commander, telling him about this morning's meeting.

After gathering everything he needed to fill out the forms required to close out the Barret case, he began at the top, with the case report narrative. He pushed to accomplish as much as possible this morning. So he didn't look up until his cellphone vibrated.

It was 8:00. He switched gears and texted Commander Lincoln. He asked to meet after his and Martin's 10:00 meeting to discuss the options. He knew he might be putting the commander on the spot, but he needed to move forward.

He'd just set his phone back on his desk when it vibrated again. Lincoln texted he'd be in his office until he heard from Pete.

Smiling in satisfaction, he returned to the case report narrative. He stopped at 9:25 and hurried out to the parking lot to meet Martin.

THIRTY-FIVE
Beth Rice

True to form, Martin arrived at 9:27, and they headed downtown. On a Saturday morning, the only demand for parking places was several blocks south and east of the Golden Rule Building, near the farmers' market. Martin pulled into a convenient spot on 7th Place, and the two men climbed the stairs to the mezzanine level and the coffee shop. They ordered Diet Cokes and sat at a table with an unobstructed view of the entrance.

Beth's fast-paced arrival brought a smile to their faces. She saw them but got a cup of coffee before sitting down.

"Do I need to plead the fifth or request that an attorney be assigned free of charge?" She chuckled.

"Every attorney I know would advise all of the above," Pete said, looking serious. "We, on the other hand, think you'll be sorry if you do."

"Heaven knows I'm already sorry about enough things, sweetie, so what do you need?"

Pete had set the photo lineup he'd created face down on the table in front of him. Before showing it to her, he said, "Beth, this is really important. We think the wrong person may have been convicted of the attack you saw on the mezzanine level ten years ago. We created a

213

photo lineup. We'd like you to look at it and tell us if the man you described to us on Wednesday is one of these people. There's no need to rush. It's important that you're certain. If you're not, or none of these people is the person you saw that day, that's fine. It's been a long time. The only thing that's important is that if you select one of these people, you're certain."

"How long did you rehearse that?" Beth laughed.

"All night. I got next to no sleep." Pete smiled.

"Let me see it, dear."

Pete handed the photo lineup to her, and she looked at the nine photos ... for a total of about two seconds before she said, "It's him. Top row far right. They all have the birthmark I mentioned—although I see one is the wrong color. Are you checking to see if I'm color blind?" she teased.

"I know it's the guy on the top right because of his eyes. See how close together they are? And see how the right one seems to be looking off a touch to the left, like he's ever so slightly cross-eyed? Also, he barely has any lips. I remember that too. If he was a woman, lipstick might help that."

"You remember all of that from ten years ago?" Pete asked.

"I do, because I thought I was looking at evil personified. Who else would attack an elderly woman the way he did? Seeing him, and knowing there was nothing I could do to stop him, burned a photo of his face into my brain. You may be wondering why, in that case, I didn't follow up on it after I returned. It's because Mom died while I was staying with her. I was grieving when I came back and for quite some time afterwards. I had trouble caring about much of anything."

"Just in case, want to take another, slow look at each of those men?" Martin asked.

"I will, because it's obvious you want me to."

Beth propped her head on her right hand and studied the lineup for a minute. Then she looked up and said, "Top right. Definitely the guy in the top right photo. Are you going to tell me his name and how many other women he's attacked?"

"No, Beth," Pete said. "But thank you for making a special trip here this morning to help us. Can we give you a ride somewhere?"

"You sure can! I have a daughter who lives in Denver. Is that on your way, sweetie?" She chortled.

"Heck, it can't be more than a few thousand miles out of our way, if you count out and back." Pete laughed.

Beth snapped her fingers and said, "Thanks for the offer, but I forgot to bring my suitcase. I hope whatever you're up to, I was able to help, boys. Good luck and stay safe. It's not the world I grew up in."

They got her last name, Rice, as well as her address and phone numbers, and hurried back to the unmarked car.

As soon as he had his seatbelt fastened, Pete texted Lincoln. "She instantly identified the guy I selected. He's in Stillwater. Available now?"

THIRTY-SIX
Commander Lincoln

Commander Lincoln sent an immediate, one word response to Pete's text. "Yes!"

Ten minutes later, Pete and Martin walked into his office.

"Based on the evidence we've uncovered, I think there's reason to believe Edgar Waltham isn't guilty of the armed assault he was convicted of ten years ago," Pete said. He explained in detail how he and Martin stumbled across the first clue, and how the evidence grew from there. He pulled out the photo lineup they showed Beth Rice, and told how she picked Todd Trimont out immediately.

"It's been ten years," Pete said. "But she said the whole situation had such an impact on her, she never forgot his face. The thing is, Commander, the attack for which Waltham was convicted matches Trimont's MO. According to the court transcripts, the murder that has him in Stillwater now happened when he hit the woman he mugged over the head harder than he'd intended. He was arrested but not convicted for another similar case in 2008, a year before the Golden Rule Building attack. That time he got off on a technicality. Bottom line: all three crimes had the same MO and happened in St. Paul, where he resided."

"When did you find time to solve the Barrett case?" Lincoln asked.

"Well, sir, we found a spare moment here and there," Pete said.

Lincoln shook his head and said, "So what are you asking of me, Pete?"

"That you help us find a way to get the county attorney to review Waltham's conviction in hopes of getting him exonerated."

"And you think one eyewitness for a ten-year-old conviction will accomplish that?"

"No, but I hope in combination with the confessions of the people responsible for the threats to the eyewitness, it's a good start. Let me paint a scenario for you, sir. Both men were in Stillwater; Trimont still is. I'd like one of us to contact the Department of Corrections Office of Special Investigations (OSI), explain the possible wrongful conviction, and tell them we're interested in learning if Trimont has ever made statements relating to the 2009 Golden Rule incident."

"Inmates in the same cell block often know about each other's convictions and sentences," Pete continued. "They're also aware of upcoming releases. If Trimont and Waltham were in the same cell block, Trimont would have been smart to keep his mouth shut as long as Waltham was incarcerated. Why risk getting beat up or worse for being responsible for someone else being there? However, once Waltham was released, Trimont might have bragged about Waltham taking the wrap for him."

Pete rubbed the back of his neck and said, OSI monitors gang activity, informants, and gossip among the prisoners. Can we explain the situation and ask them to monitor for anything Trimont said or is saying about

Waltham or the 2009 attack in the Golden Rule Building? I think it's worthwhile."

Lincoln said, "I'm willing to contact OIS, but remember, even in combination with your supplemental reports, it might not be enough."

"I understand, but I haven't thought of anything better. Do you have any suggestions, sir?"

"A confession from Trimont might do it, but since the statute of limitations has run out, it's value too might be questioned. Like you, I hate to have a man continue to pay for a crime if he's innocent. Let me see what I can do."

After thanking Commander Lincoln, Pete and Martin returned to Pete's office, anxious to tackle the necessary reports and close out the Barrett case. While Pete worked on supplemental reports covering Sandra and Thaddeus Norcross's confessions and Beth's selection of Todd Trimont out of a photo lineup, Martin worked on his Barrett case report narrative.

Pausing, Martin looked at Pete and said, "Maybe one day soon we'll have a robot riding in the back seat, preparing all the reports as we work our way through a case."

"Be careful what you wish for. Maybe it'll also drive your unmarked car." Pete smiled.

"Ain't happening," Martin said. "Driving that car requires a special touch. They'll never program a computer capable of matching my reflexes or my intuition."

"Keep telling yourself that." Pete chuckled and went back to work.

After finishing and disseminating the supplemental reports, Pete returned to his case summary narrative.

They worked silently and without a break for two hours. Then Pete stood, stretched, and said, "How about I buy your lunch, and we finish this next week?"

"You've got my vote." Martin smiled.

"Great. Where would you like to eat?"

"How about Keys? It's close, so we won't waste time driving to and from some other restaurant."

They shut everything down, put on their suit coats, and walked out to Martin's car.

It was 77°, but the cloud cover kept Martin's car comfortable, even without the AC. He found a parking place along Robert Street, and they walked back to the light at 10th Street. Martin wished the light would hurry up and change. He hadn't said anything, but his meager breakfast didn't hold back the hunger.

He and Pete discussed the case and how it evolved as they walked back to the corner and crossed the street. He marveled at Pete's drive and stick-to-itiveness. He reveled in having Pete back at work ... and hoped nothing ever changed that.

Two or three steps from the curb on the other side of Robert, out of the corner of his eye, Pete saw it. The street noises coming from MTC buses, car engines and horns, and chattering and laughing pedestrians had masked any advanced warning of the SUV speeding toward him and Martin.

THIRTY-SEVEN
Then ...

Looking at and talking to Pete, Martin remained oblivious to the looming threat.

Pete reacted. He half lifted, half body-bumped Martin onto the sidewalk. A nano-second later and a half-step behind Martin, he felt the searing pain. The SUV's front bumper struck his right thigh. Momentum tossed him onto the hood. He rolled into the windshield, over the driver's side of the SUV, and onto the pavement.

Martin heard a roaring and squealing vehicle strike something. It happened almost simultaneously with his crashing to the sidewalk. Dazed from the impact, it took a minute to get his bearings and look for Pete.

Then he saw it. A man lay sprawled in the middle of the street, motionless.

Not Pete! Please Lord, don't let that be Pete! he thought.

"Pete," he yelled, lunging for him.

Dropping to his knees on the pavement, Martin bent forward, getting his face next to Pete's while he carefully checked for a pulse. Then he whispered, "Hang in there, Pete. You just saved my life. People who love you are counting on you. Stay with me."

Gently resting his hand on Pete's shoulder, maintaining the frail connection, Martin pulled his radio from his belt and reported, "Officer down! Officer down! We need EMS now! Traffic accident. Officer struck. Severe injuries. Request medics to intersection of 10th and Robert streets. Suspect vehicle fleeing north on Robert at high rate of speed."

He'd barely set his radio on the pavement, noticed pedestrians directing traffic, and returned to talking to Pete when he heard the sirens. He hoped and prayed that the paramedics and EMTs could save Pete.

He neither moved nor looked anywhere but at Pete. Still touching Pete's shoulder ever so lightly, he continued repeating, "Stay with me, Pete, come on, stay with me," while a series of prayers ran through his head.

Suddenly, Pete's eyes opened. He looked at Martin and asked, "What happened?" Then, without warning, his eyes closed. He didn't react to Martin's questions.

Time stood still for Martin as he remained alongside Pete, trying not to despair. It wasn't easy. He hoped and prayed his presence didn't mean only that Pete wouldn't be alone when he died.

Then he heard shouts and the sound of running feet. Two EMTs from the St. Paul Fire Department, located a block away, didn't wait for the ambulance. They ran all out to him and Pete.

Reluctantly, Martin relinquished his space to the EMTs. "He saved my life," he told the man and woman. "That should be me down there."

Police, fire, and ambulance sirens competed for dominance. EMTs secured the area. Police officers pushed back onlookers and obtained names and contact information, as well as descriptions of the vehicle, the driver, and any passengers.

Perhaps in reaction to the touch of the newly arrived paramedics, Pete's eyes opened again. This time, they stayed open. But he seemed disoriented when they spoke to him.

"TBI," a paramedic said.

"Meaning?" Martin asked.

"Traumatic brain injury. They'll probably do a CT scan when we get him to Regions."

Another paramedic radioed into the Regions ER that Pete had a pulse, and his breathing was labored. A fracture to his right femur was likely. He suffered a concussion with brief loss of consciousness. "Labored breathing indicates possible broken or cracked ribs. There's a road rash on his left cheek from when he landed on the pavement." The paramedic called for spinal immobilization and transport to Regions.

Martin suppressed his desire to ask why it was taking so long. He knew his anxiety probably made it seem far longer than it actually was. He calmed down a bit when they let him ride in the back of the ambulance with Pete.

When they reached the Regions ER, a trauma team was waiting for them. They transferred Pete to a trauma bed for assessment, X-rays, and stabilization. Then they'd take him to surgery or the ICU.

Meanwhile, Martin sat in the waiting area. First, he called Katie. He assured her that Pete would be fine and hoped it was true. He explained Pete would probably need to spend a few days in the hospital. "I'm on my way," she said, sounding far more put together than Martin felt. He told her he was in the ER waiting area and would be there when she arrived.

Then he called Commander Lincoln.

Lincoln didn't request any details. Martin wondered why, but didn't ask. Lincoln said he was on his way. He meant it. Five minutes later, Martin saw him walk in and scan the room. He stood and waved to get Lincoln's attention.

Joining Martin, Lincoln asked, "How's he doing?"

"Based on what the paramedics said, sounds like he has a concussion and a broken leg. He might also have some cracked or broken ribs. The paramedic said that might be why he groaned when they moved him."

"How about you, Martin?"

"That should be me in there, Commander. He got me out of the path of the speeding vehicle, instead of protecting himself. He has a baby. He should have taken care of himself first."

"Can you actually imagine Pete doing that?"

"Well, no."

"Nor I. He's strong and determined. Between Katie and the baby, he has all the motivation he'll need."

"Sir, do you really believe that?"

"Yes, and I'll continue until I have a good reason to stop."

"We arrested the driver and his passenger," Lincoln continued. "They're sixteen-year-old punks. They'd just stolen the SUV and were on their way to a chop shop."

"Your call triggered an immediate BOLO. Bystanders described the vehicle as a blue Chevrolet Equinox. They also described the driver and his passenger. They were pulled over within fifteen minutes. The Equinox had damage to the right front bumper and the spiderweb crack in the windshield."

"Did you notify his wife?" Lincoln asked.

"Yes. She's on her way."

Katie arrived in time to hear the doctor's report on Pete's injuries. He had a concussion, but a CT scan ruled out a brain bleed as well as internal injuries. An X-ray showed the femur on his right leg was shattered, and an orthopedic surgeon was on the way to insert a rod or a plate. Another X-ray showed two cracked ribs. He concluded by mentioning they'd cleaned up and treated the road rash on Pete's left cheek.

"Running and downhill skiing are important parts of his life," Katie said. "I'm afraid he'll be inconsolable if he can't do both. He'll be able to, won't he?"

"Assuming all goes well with the insertion of a rod in his right leg, and there's no reason to think it won't, the two most important ingredients are desire and determination. With a large dose of each, he should be back doing both in about six months."

"In that case," Katie said, "there's nothing to worry about."

"He's an investigator with the St. Paul Police," Commander Lincoln said. "Same estimate for when he'll be able to return to work? We need him."

The doctor nodded and, looking at Martin and Lincoln, he said, "You can see him, briefly."

Turning his attention to Katie, he said, "You can stay with him until they take him into surgery. He's going to be groggy," he added. "We gave him something for the pain."

"How about our son?" Katie asked, nodding at Teddy.

"Taking him in to see his dad is fine, but we prefer the baby doesn't stay until we take your husband into surgery. Can someone take him after a few minutes?"

Almost before the doctor completed that question, Martin said, "I'd like to do that."

Katie smiled at him and said, "Teddy will like it too."

She and Teddy were the first to see Pete.

Seeing them, he broke into a pained smile and reached for Katie.

She moved in close, bent, and kissed his forehead. Then she held Teddy close enough for Pete to lift his head an inch or two and kiss him, but not close enough for anything but Teddy's hand to touch the unbandaged side of his dad's face. As soon as Teddy touched Pete, he babbled and giggled.

"You'll be fine," she whispered. "I held my breath when Martin called. I remember the other time he called. That was after you were shot. I love you, Pete."

"So glad I could see you before surgery. It means a lot. Afraid I'll compound your workload when I get home. It'll be like having two babies. I'm sorry, Katie."

"Sorry? Pete, Martin told me you saved his life."

"I'm not sorry for that. I am sorry I wasn't just one step faster."

"I'm just glad you weren't one step slower. You've always been a hero in my book, Pete. All that matters now is that you're alive and you'll come home to us. Let me get Martin. He's anxious to see you. He's a mess ... emotionally, I mean."

"Please, get him, Katie. I know Martin. I know he feels responsible. Help me convince him he isn't."

Katie ducked out long enough to get Martin.

When he saw Pete, tears welled up in Martin's eyes. Through the tears, he said, "I'm so sorry, Pete. It's all my fault. How could I have been so oblivious to what was happening?"

"I was looking at you, Martin. That's why I saw the SUV. You were looking at me. It must be my fault. I'm the one who suggested going to lunch at 1:00. Had we gone at noon or 1:30, it wouldn't have happened. Next time, Martin, you're taking the hit."

Martin couldn't help it. He smiled crookedly.

"Don't worry, Martin. You'll be paying for this. I just dumped closing out the Barrett case in your lap. I think I've done about as much as I can when it comes to Edgar Waltham. It's in Commander Lincoln's and the county attorney's hands."

"Commander Lincoln is waiting to see you," Katie and Martin said simultaneously, and Martin added, "He gave the doctor the impression we can't make it without you. I agree, Pete. Let me take Teddy, Katie, and I'll send the commander in."

Commander Lincoln walked in with his usual aplomb and said, "Evidently you've decided you need an extended vacation every six months. Next time, find a better way to make your point. Don't worry about anything except getting well. We'll handle everything, including doing our best to work a miracle for Edgar Waltham. I'm proud of you, Pete. Keep me apprised of your progress."

Pete saluted, carefully, and said, "Thanks for everything, Commander."

Lincoln smiled and said, "Knock off the salutes, Pete," and left.

Katie stood as close as she could to Pete and held his hand while they prepared him for surgery. She looked the other way when they inserted the IVs. When they wheeled him into surgery, she joined Martin and Teddy in the waiting area.

Seeing Teddy on Martin's lap, gurgling, giggling, and smiling at the faces and the noises Martin made, she laughed and asked, "Which of you is the adult?"

"Physically or mentally?" Martin grinned.

Martin kept her company during Pete's surgery. After two hours, he saw her anxiety escalate with each passing minute. Teddy lay sound asleep in her arms, providing no distraction. Searching his brain for diversions, Martin got an idea. "Want to call Pete's parents and Grandma Jackie?" he asked. Amid the chaos, doing that hadn't occurred to either of them.

"Could you do that for me, Martin? Right now, I'm not feeling brave enough."

"I can, but I'm sure they'd like to talk to you. It'll help pass the time. Try not to let the time the surgery is taking alarm you. Remember, they said his femur was shattered. That must take a while to fix. Plus, they can't sew him up before the super glue dries." He saw nothing funny about the surgery or Pete's injuries, but he was determined to help Katie through this.

"Oh Martin," she said, nudging him with her elbow. "What would we do without you?"

"I'm not planning on you having to find out," he said and rubbed her back.

She handed Teddy to Martin, moved to a more secluded spot, and pulled out her phone.

Pete's mom answered. At Katie's request, his dad picked up another phone, so she could speak with them simultaneously. "I'm calling about Pete," she began and heard a gasp. "He'll be fine," she assured them. "He's in the hospital. He was struck by an SUV but, again, he'll be fine. He's in surgery right now."

"We saw on the news that a police officer was struck by an SUV in downtown St. Paul," his dad said. "Was that Pete?"

"I'm afraid so."

"They said the driver of the speeding SUV was arrested," Theo added. "Every time we hear about an incident involving a St. Paul police officer, we cringe. We know we're overreacting, because of the number of officers out there, but it's spontaneous."

"Believe me," Katie said, "I understand." As she said that, she saw Martin stand and motion to her. A man dressed in scrubs had entered the room, and Martin moved toward him. "Hang on Mom and Dad," she said. "I think we're about to get a report from Pete's surgeon. I'll put you on speaker so you can hear him. Don't worry if you can't hear everything. As soon as he finishes talking to Martin and me, I'll come back on the phone with you."

The surgeon reported that the surgery was a success, and Pete came through it well. "I have no trouble differentiating those who stay in shape from those who don't," he added. "He's in excellent physical condition. That should help speed his recovery. But due to the severity of the break, he'll need a lot of physical therapy, and it will still be about eight weeks before he can walk without a cane. I recommend a wheelchair for at least the first four weeks, due as much to the fractured ribs as his shattered femur. Both crutches and a cane will strain the fractured ribs and cause a little to a lot of pain."

"He's in recovery. You'll be able to see him in about a half hour."

"When will he be released?" Katie asked.

"In five days to a week, if all goes well and you're able to manage with him."

"I'm glad you didn't say manage him." She smiled. "Right now, the thing that worries me the most is trying to get him to use a wheelchair. I know he'll have trouble feeling and looking so dependent."

The surgeon said, "For the first month, I think the pain that would accompany any other way of getting around will solve the problem for you."

Katie discussed the surgeon's report with Pete's parents, then mentioned Grandma Jackie. "Would you like me to call her or do you prefer to handle it?" she asked.

"I think it's better if Mother is not alone when she hears," Pete's mom said. "I'll drive over there now. Do you think Pete will be able to have visitors this evening?"

Katie suggested they wait an hour or two. "That'll be between 7:00 and 8:00," she said. "They should have moved him from recovery to intensive care by then. He'll spend tonight there, because he has a concussion. They want to keep an eye on him."

They thanked her for calling and said they hoped to see her tonight. Katie had almost disconnected when she heard Pete's mom call her name. "Where is Teddy?" she asked.

"Here with me."

"Can we bring him home with us tonight, in case you decide to spend the night with Pete?"

Katie had wondered if she could ask Martin to do that and appreciated the offer. "But I don't have enough diapers to last until morning, nor his sleepers, et cetera, et cetera, and on and on," she sighed.

"We have a key, remember? We'll stop by your place before coming home. Everything will be fine. We'll enjoy spending some extra time with Theo's namesake. Don't worry about a thing, Katie."

Katie heard the smile in her voice and said, "You're wonderful, Mom and Dad. Thanks so much." They were her in-laws, but she'd always called them Mom and Dad. She didn't think she could feel closer to them if they had a blood connection. She hung up and thanked God for Pete's family.

Martin put an arm around her and squeezed her shoulder.

Teddy slept through all of it.

Katie almost ran to Pete's side when a nurse said she could visit him in recovery.

He smiled as soon as he saw her and asked her to take him home.

"Soon," she said. "Relax. Before long, they'll move you to a room."

While Pete was in post-op recovery, she stayed with him whenever permitted. During that time, she sat on a chair pulled in as close as she could get to him. She held his hand. That way, whether his eyes were open or closed, he knew she was there, and she spoke softly about anything that came to mind.

Meanwhile, Pete drifted in and out of consciousness.

Due to the restrictions on visiting time while he was in recovery, Martin stayed in the waiting area with Teddy. Without waking the baby, he called Michelle a second time. He updated her on the surgery and the prognosis.

At 7:30, they transferred Pete to the ICU. The other bed in his room wasn't occupied. That gave them a little leeway when it came to visitors. Katie and Teddy went to see him, then Martin. Martin again said he wished they could trade places.

"You always were a glory seeker," Pete said.

Martin noticed how Pete winced whenever he moved one iota.

"Martin," Pete said, "we never got lunch."

Nor dinner, Martin thought. But his stomach was still too iffy to consider eating anything.

When Pete's parents and Grandma Jackie arrived, Martin took over as the chief babysitter. He knew from their eyes that Pete's mom and Grandma Jackie had been crying. He gave them and Pete's dad a group hug, with Teddy in the middle, giggling.

After their visit, he walked Pete's parents and grandma to their car in the parking ramp. Then he called Michelle to say he was on his way ... a good five hours later than originally planned.

Katie, Teddy, Martin, Pete's parents, and Grandma Jackie spent the next four days rotating who was with him. Of course, most of the time went to Katie.

She was surprised how dependent the fractured ribs made him. He winced with each twist or turn, no matter how insignificant. He never cried out, but she believed that it took extra effort.

On day five, she and Teddy arrived at the hospital with a wheelchair, walker, and cane in the trunk, convinced she faced a long four to six months, even though it would be nice to have Pete home.

"We did it!" Pete said when he saw Katie and Teddy.

"Never doubted for a second that you would, Pete."

"Are you sure you're up to the challenge the next four to six months will present? I'm afraid my total dependence on you will grow old ... in about ten minutes. Can you cope with a grouchier me? Unfortunately, I can guarantee it'll happen and it won't be pleasant. I know that much about myself."

"It's understandable, Pete. I'm not sure it would be any different if we traded places," she said and carefully kissed him deeply.

THIRTY-EIGHT
One More Detail

Tuesday, December 21, 2019, Pete and Katie had their home decorated for Teddy's first Christmas as Pete began his third month of medical leave. Though he thoroughly enjoyed the added time with Katie and Teddy, he missed the exhilaration that accompanied being immersed in a case. For that reason, he attacked his rigorous regime of exercise and physical therapy with dogged determination.

Awaiting the arrival of Charlie Odin, the St. Paul Fire Department's Assistant Chief of Emergency Medical Services, Pete was hopeful and excited. He and Charlie were on a mission, and Pete couldn't wait to get things rolling.

This morning, Pete's boss, Senior Commander Lincoln, set things in motion when he brought the paperwork to Pete. Tonight Pete and Charlie hoped to wrap things up.

When the doorbell rang right on schedule at 7:10, Pete smiled at Katie. He'd just graduated from crutches to a cane, so he stood, grasped his new, Irish-plaid cane, and walked cautiously alongside Katie to the front door.

Charlie beamed and said, "Glad to see you're back on your feet. My buddies and I are tracking your progress via Martin and the grapevine. I don't know if I'm more excited or nervous about tonight. How about you, Pete?"

"Ditto. His sister Elaine is expecting me, but I didn't mention you. Decided I should wait and see how he reacts when he sees me. His sister assured me he'll be there. She doesn't plan to say anything about me stopping by."

Charlie nodded and said, "I pulled in as close as I could to the garage door without kissing it. It's slippery everywhere—except on your driveway. Does your guardian angel get time-and-a-half overtime?"

"We have Katie to thank for that." Pete chuckled. "She's doing everything possible to get me back to work ASAP. That includes making sure I don't fall and undo everything I've accomplished thus far, thanks to a large dose of help from her. Let's avoid the steps by going through the garage."

Pete proceeded gingerly to Charlie's car, unwilling to risk undoing even an iota of his hard-earned progress. Then he carefully lowered himself into the passenger seat.

Charlie chatted all the way to St. Paul's Frogtown neighborhood. The topics included how things were going with Pete's recuperation and when he thought he'd be back to work.

"I'm shooting for mid- to late-March, but I might have to climb over Katie to get to the car." Pete laughed.

They also discussed how they'd proceed once they reached their destination.

"What kind of a reaction are you anticipating?" Charlie asked.

"Amazement or maybe disbelief."

Reaching their destination, they shuffled across the sheet of ice that stretched from the car to the apartment building. Then, out of deference to Pete, they took the elevator to the third floor. From the hallway, they heard the sound of a TV coming from Elaine's apartment.

In keeping with Pete's plan, Odin stood several paces down the hall while Pete knocked.

Seconds later, they both heard the deadbolt.

Elaine opened the door and ushered Pete in. She didn't notice Charlie.

So far so good, Pete thought.

Just inside the door, Elaine whispered, "Another tough week, and he's exhausted. So please understand if he isn't as happy as he should be. Okay, here goes," she said and walked over to the couch where Edgar was sprawled out with his back to them, dozing.

Tapping him on the shoulder, she said, "Ed, there's someone here to speak with you."

Edgar grunted, sat up, struggled to his feet, and turned to face the visitor. Seeing Pete, his face lit up and he said, "You're our hero, Commander Culnane. Zach thinks the world of you. Zach, Elaine, and I all appreciate everything you did to try to clear my name." Nodding at Pete's cane he added, "I hope that isn't a result of those efforts."

"No, but this is," Pete said, pulling an envelope from his jacket pocket. "The first few paragraphs say it all."

Looking puzzled, Edgar removed the pages from the envelope and scanned the first one. When he looked up, his eyes were moist, and he said, "I know this took a lot of effort." His voice cracked as he added, "It means the world to me … and my family."

"When Martin's and my investigation cast doubt on the validity of your conviction, Edgar, we were compelled to seek justice. That's the reason we're in this business. We couldn't let it pass. When I was sidelined, my boss, Commander Lincoln, picked up the ball and took it into the end zone."

"The guy who actually attacked the woman in the Golden Rule Building helped," Pete added. "Knowing the statute of limitations had run out, he couldn't keep his mouth shut. Right after your release, he began bragging to anyone who'd listen that you'd just finished serving his sentence."

Pete smiled and added, "I'm delighted that with a lot of help we succeeded in getting you exonerated. Wish we could have accomplished this a decade ago. Martin wanted to be here when I told you, but he's tied up with a new case and didn't want to delay this meeting."

Smiling broadly and looking energized Edgar said, "I can't believe you succeeded. Maybe now I can go back to the work I love."

"Hang on," Pete said, opened the door, and waved Charlie in.

Seeing Charlie, Edgar's jaw dropped.

"Charlie's been doing some research," Pete said. "Any chance Edgar can get a job with the SPFD, Charlie?"

"That's why I'm here. We've missed you, Ed. Would you consider coming back to work for me? I've already cleared things with the chief. One of your buddies is retiring in January, so we'll have a slot for you."

Clearing his throat, Edgar said softly, "You have no idea how much I've wanted to come back to work for you and hated not being able to do the job I love."

Then, smiling broadly, he asked, "When can I start?"

Charlie smiled and asked, "How about the first of February?"

Elaine hugged Edgar and the tears flowed . . . for both of them.

ACKNOWLEDGMENTS

My thanks to Pam McCord, Valerie Olson, Kris Olson, Jen Smith, Pat Harper, Sean Harper, and Diane Pearson for their research assistance.

I'm also grateful to Ruth Krueger, Deb Harper, and Marly Cornell for their proofreading and editorial expertise. Special thanks to Christopher Smith for sharing his time and computer expertise and being an invaluable creative resource at every step.

Other books by S.L. Smith

Blinded by the Sight
Running Scared
Murder on a Stick
Mistletoe and Murder
Murder on Cathedral Hill
Last Breath
Dead Reckoning
A Party to Murder
The Trigger
Malice

www.ingramcontent.com/pod-product-compliance
Lightning Source LLC
Chambersburg PA
CBHW060552260626
47161CB00003B/1159